THE CURSE OF THE VIPER KING

RUSSELL JAMES

SEVERED PRESS
HOBART TASMANIA

THE CURSE OF THE VIPER KING

ISBN: 978-1-925840-19-3

For D,
You saved me from a rattlesnake, and look what that experience spawned.

CHAPTER ONE

Taking this job had been the worst mistake of Emiliano's life.

That fact grew clearer each day. Cutting timber in the Amazon hadn't been the adventure he'd thought it would be. He slept in a hammock under a thatched roof with nineteen other men. Food ranged from bad all the way down to inedible. Even after sunset, the temperature never dipped below incinerating and the humidity threatened to suffocate him. The work was tough, the biting insects tougher.

Then there were the nights. Darker than any he'd ever experienced. The creepy animal noises from the rainforest and the impenetrable blackness stoked primal fears he thought he'd left behind under his childhood bed. This logging camp made him wonder how many stories of Amazonian monsters were actually true. Many days he doubted he was any better off than he'd been in the Sao Paulo barrio shack he'd abandoned.

This morning, men worked around the edge of the several hectare clear cut, swinging axes and wielding chainsaws. Near the center stood a pile of scrap timber and debris. Bruno, a stout man in baggy shorts and a tattered red T-shirt wore the tanks of a flamethrower on his back. He aimed the wand at the debris and sent a stream of orange fire into the heart of the pile. It burst into flame.

Emiliano finished filling his chainsaw with gas and screwed the gas cap back on. Fuel leaked from the carburetor's base and created a shiny trail down the saw's side. The chemical stink combined with the oppressive heat made his head swim. He stood up and shook it off.

"Gabriel, come on," he said.

His younger brother approached with a chainsaw resting on his shoulder. Two years younger but four inches taller, with a shaved head and broad shoulders, the muscle shirt he wore exposed strong biceps and a simple five-pointed star on a heavy chain around his neck. Gabriel should have been intimidating as hell. But mentally, he'd never gotten past eight years old, and Emiliano had been looking out for him ever since. Recruiting his brother, his last living relative, for this adventure had seemed a necessity. He'd been afraid to leave Gabriel behind to fend for himself. Now he was afraid he'd led him into a jungle hell instead.

Emiliano pointed to a huge mahogany tree at the clearing's edge. "That one's ours. You ready?"

Gabriel gave one of his goofy grins, made even more comical by his crooked teeth. "Okay, Mili."

Emiliano wished he deserved the complete trust Gabriel bestowed on him, but after getting them into this mess…

"I'll go high, you go low," Emiliano said. He judged which way the tree would fall, then pointed to where he wanted Gabriel to start cutting.

Gabriel went to the other side of the tree. They both yanked their chainsaws to life and sent the teeth biting into the dense wood. Two rooster tails of shavings sprayed through the air.

The mahogany surrendered slowly to the saws. Gabriel's saw bit too hard and stalled. He worked it back out of the slot he'd cut.

But he'd done enough. Emiliano drove his saw deep. A wedge of wood dropped out of the trunk. Emiliano extracted the saw. The tree began to buckle at the cut.

Then, meters away from the trunk, the roots at the far side began to pull from the ground. The tree leaned in the opposite direction of the cut. Its shadow swept across the ground and landed on Gabriel like a sniper's crosshairs. Gabriel stood oblivious in the dark stripe, trying to restart his saw.

"Gabriel!" Emiliano dropped his saw and charged his brother. He gripped Gabriel's waist in his headlong rush and drove him away from the falling tree's path. Gabriel dropped his saw as Emiliano drove him to the ground.

The tree smashed to the ground with the staccato crackle of snapping branches. It missed their feet by millimeters and sprayed a shower of dirt all across their legs. The trunk crushed Gabriel's saw and the stink of gasoline and oil polluted the air in an instant. The echo of the crash rolled away and left the clearing dead silent.

Other workers sent up a cry. Men from around the clearing sprinted to Emiliano and Gabriel. Emiliano shook his brother.

"Are you okay?"

Gabriel grasped the star around his neck with one hand. He wiped some dirt from his mouth and nodded. "I think so." He looked over at his crushed chainsaw. "The boss will not be happy about that."

Emiliano got to his feet and swept some leaves from his hair. He helped his brother up.

A worker arrived at the tree and cried out in terror.

The fallen tree displayed a fan of dirt-clotted roots like a peacock's tail. They exposed a sheet of gray stone underneath. Emiliano stepped around for a closer look.

Embedded in the rock was the fossilized skeleton of a giant snake, with huge fangs and a head nearly a meter long.

The man who'd screamed stepped away from the stone. Others arrived and jerked to a stop beside him, as if the fossil emitted some repellent force.

"It's a demon," one man whispered.

"Creature of Hell," another said.

Gabriel looked over Emiliano's shoulder. He grabbed his brother's elbow. "Is that a demon?"

"I don't know."

"Are there more like it still around?"

Emiliano certainly hoped not.

CHAPTER TWO

Four years ago

The tarp covering the desert excavation created a parallelogram of shade, but it made no difference. Dr. Grant Coleman still felt like he had a front seat to a blast furnace. But if his team could get this Allosaurus skull out of the sandstone in one piece, the discomfort would be well worth the reward.

At Grant's feet, three sunburned graduate students in T-shirts and frayed shorts worked at the fossil with dental picks and brushes.

"This is so slow," one of them whined. "We've been digging this out a millimeter at a time for days."

"It's been there for a few million years," Grant said. "There's really no hurry to do it improperly."

"But seriously, this is so…mind numbing."

"Because you aren't savoring the thrill of discovery," Grant said in over-the-top dramatics. "The excitement of being the first set of human eyes to see what you're bringing to light. Here you are, in the solitude and silence of the desert. It's just you and a former apex predator."

"You have to admit," another student said. "The heat and all is a little draining."

"But there are no insects, no drenching rains, and the air wicks away sweat in an instant. You can't always pick and choose where to do paleontology, but when I can, I pick the desert. You wouldn't catch me dead in a jungle."

Grant left the excavation and joined Hannah, one of his most promising students as she searched a rock wall for signs of their next big find. Multi-colored layers of sediment ran like wavy lines across the stone. A broad, floppy hat shielded her pale face from the sun.

"Anything promising?" he asked.

"Not yet."

She sidestepped left without looking. Something rattled at her feet.

A rattlesnake lay coiled in the sun between two rocks. Its raised head pointed at the two of them. Its rattle stood erect and vibrated its chilling warning.

Hannah froze. Grant's pulse spiked. He gripped Hannah's shoulders.

"Nice and easy," he whispered. "Step straight back with me."

She followed his lead as an awkward dance partner. One, two, three, four synchronized steps backwards. The rattling stopped. The snake lowered its head.

"Oh my God," Hannah whispered. "I didn't see that snake at all. That was so close."

"Too close. Rule of thumb: give a snake all the room it wants."

"Wow." She looked up at him in admiration. "You stayed pretty cool around that snake."

"I've seen a lot of them in the desert. You get used to them."

In reality, sweat ran down his spine and his heart hadn't slowed down yet. Snakes gave him the creeps, with their slick scales and their penetrating slit irises. He hoped Hannah wouldn't notice the tremble in his hands. He transitioned the discussion into a moment of instruction.

"In the past, they got much bigger than that. There are documented snake fossils over ten meters long and over a meter wide."

"I'd hate to stumble across one of those."

"So would I. Lucky for us we missed their heyday by millions of years." He directed Hannah to the right. "Let's check the sediments a little further over here."

He glanced back at the snake. Its forked tongue whipped in and out of its mouth. It didn't blink.

He decided he could go years without seeing another snake up close, and that would be just fine.

CHAPTER THREE

Present day

Grant slapped an insect on his cheek. He checked his palm and saw a splat of blood. The Amazon jungle was turning out to be everything he'd thought he'd hate, and more. He dipped his paddle back into the river and kept the canoe moving downstream.

"There are more insects down here than up on the plateau, no?" Janaina Silva said.

"Yes, but at least they're smaller."

Grant and Janaina were the sole survivors of an expedition to an unknown plateau in the far reaches of Amazonia. They had battled an Ankylosaurus, pterosaurs, and giant ants. They'd barely escaped with their lives, climbed down to the river, and begun a long downstream paddle they'd hoped would get them back to civilization. Back in the United States, Grant was a professor of paleontology and a horror novelist. Janaina was an environmentalist and advocate for native peoples' rights here in Brazil.

The humidity seemed to sap every bit of energy from Grant. Sweat rolled down the sides of his face. His arms ached from paddling.

The canoe navigated a curve in the river. A sandbar appeared up ahead, an unnatural white between the rich greens of the jungle and the river's tannin-brown.

"That would be a safe place," Janaina said. "Perhaps we take a break, stretch our legs."

"Hey, you know that I'm good for another hundred miles, easy. But if *you* need a break, then we should certainly take one."

Janaina flashed a bright white smile. "You are so kind to be putting my needs first."

Grant pulled in his paddle and sagged in the seat. "Well, it's all about the team effort."

Janaina steered the canoe onto the sandbar. It nosed in and Grant stepped out. After a few hours folded up, his legs took some coaxing to keep him erect. He finally rose to his full height. The younger Janaina hopped out without effort.

"No need to show off," he muttered to himself.

Janaina pulled her dark hair out of its pony tail and gave it a shake. It brushed her shoulders. The week of outdoor adventure had bronzed her skin. Grant had just burned.

"I have to confess something," Grant said. "Fighting the dinosaurs up above the clouds? That wasn't my first rodeo."

Janaina drew her hair back into a pony tail. "That was not a rodeo. I have been to the Festa do Peão de Barretos. I have seen a rodeo."

"Sorry, that's an American phrase. I meant to say that last week wasn't my first encounter with giant creatures the world thought were extinct."

"Now I think you are, how you say, pulling my foot."

"That's pulling your leg, and no, I'm not. Over a year ago, I was recruited to explore a cavern in Montana that had been sealed for thousands of years. Inside, we discovered giant scorpions, a giant bat, and a host of other species that hadn't ever encountered modern man."

"Such a discovery should have made you famous, no?"

"The cavern flooded and all the evidence was destroyed."

"Wait, wasn't that event what you wrote your little scary novel about?"

"Yes, it was. And that non-fiction fiction did make me a bit famous. Famous enough that the late Ms. Katsoros recruited me for our adventure with the pterosaurs because she knew the story was true."

"Ah, so that is why of all the paleontologists in the world, TransUnion hired you."

"That and I work cheap. As an example, I'm not even charging them for the days we are going to spend here paddling down river."

"You are quite magnanimous."

"Just one of my many faults." Grant stretched his back. It creaked. "Now I don't want you thinking I'm some kind of giant monster magnet. My first experience was a fluke, and the second time someone else brought me to them on purpose. I have complete confidence that we will get downriver without encountering any mythical monsters."

"That is good. We will just keep the list of worries to pit vipers, anacondas, crocodiles, piranha fish, jaguars, and a dozen painful or poisonous insects."

"That list makes the pterosaurs look kind of good."

"We can paddle back upstream if you'd like."

"Nah, been there, done that. We'll stick with snakes and jaguars. Normal sized."

"If we stay on this sandbar much longer," Janaina said, "we'll see crocodiles. This is a prime sunning spot."

Grant hopped for the canoe. "No need to tell me that twice. I'm at my big reptile quota for the week."

They pushed the canoe back out into the river. As he prepared to step in, Grant noticed water seeping into the bottom through a split in the old wood.

"Whoa! Wait!" He pulled the canoe back onto the sandbar. Grant lifted his end out of the water. A hairline crack ran along the seam between the two sides. "This isn't going to get us home."

Janaina scanned the river bank. "Wait…I saw…there!" She pointed upstream. "We need to go there."

Grant thought they'd get that far before sinking. They boarded the canoe and paddled to the river bank. His estimate of their seaworthiness was way off. More water seeped through the crack on the way over. A lot more.

"There had better be a solution here," he said, "because that was this canoe's last trip."

"There is one right here," Janaina stepped out of the canoe and over to a rough-barked tree with narrow, waxy, green leaves. "Wild rubber."

She took off her belt and used the prong in the buckle's center to gouge a descending line across the trunk. The wound slowly filled with milky sap.

"We will patch the split. Mother Nature provides."

The sap drew slowly. It was almost an hour before they had enough to fill the crack. Janaina caught the sap and applied it to the canoe's wound with some leaves.

"That may stop the leak, but not the split," Grant said. "Hand me your belt."

Janaina gave him her belt. He took off his own and joined them together. He looped them around the stern of the canoe and cinched them tight. The crack closed up and squirted rubber sap from the tightened split.

"That ought to hold it," Grant said. He didn't sound as certain as he'd planned to.

He prayed it would last to the river's end, wherever that was. They relaunched the canoe, and headed downriver into the unknown.

CHAPTER FOUR

An hour later, Grant spotted a tendril of black smoke rising from the jungle downstream.

"I'm going to hope that is civilization up ahead," Grant said.

Janaina stopped paddling. "It is too early."

"It's never too early to be rescued."

"No, I mean to say that this is protected land. There should not be any civilization here."

"There shouldn't have been dinosaurs on the plateau either, but that happened. I'm willing to roll with this one as well."

The canoe rounded a bend and a stretch of the riverbank had been cleared. The earth down to the river had been pounded flat. The clearing stretched at least two hectares back into the jungle. Three simple, plywood shacks with small porches stood along one side, beside them a huge silver tank on short legs. At the far end, the remains of a big bonfire burned, tended by a small, dark man in a pair of basketball shorts. Behind him rose what looked like a huge, palm-thatched car port. Empty hammocks hung from posts like black cobwebs.

But the thing that sent Grant's heart soaring was the old shallow-draft barge pulled up by the shore, half-loaded with cut trees. That could be a ride out of here.

"Yes!" Grant said. "People!"

"Not people," Janaina corrected. "Loggers."

"I know you've had bad experiences with them in the past. Let's meet in the middle and agree they are humans. Humans with a way to get home."

They beached the canoe and headed for the shacks. A man in his late 30s stepped out onto the porch. He wore a tan safari-style short sleeve shirt. His dark hair touched his shirt collar. He squinted at the two of them and looked surprised. He trotted over to them.

"The only way y'all are here is if y'all are lost," he said. His voice had a long Southern drawl.

Grant sighed with relief at the familiar accent. "You have that right."

The man extended a hand. "Chad Walker. I'm running this operation for Empresa de Madeiras Cruz do Sul. That translates to 'timber company'."

Grant shook his hand. "I'm Dr. Grant Coleman, Robeson University. Don't let the smell fool you. I do teach college."

Grant turned to Janaina. "This is Jan—"

"Janice Tucker," Janaina said. "Dr. Coleman's assistant." She shook Walker's hand.

Grant realized that he and Janaina hadn't agreed on a cover story for why they were lost in Amazonia. He hoped she would follow his lead.

"We were on a paleontology expedition up stream, looking for dinosaur fossils," Grant said. "Rains flooded the camp, swept out all our communication and supplies."

"We even lost what few fossils we'd collected," Janaina added. "We're so happy to have found you."

Grant smiled. She'd followed his lead quite nicely.

"Sorry there ain't much to offer," Walker said. "The whole group here's twenty loggers, me, and my botanist, who's out scouting trees somewhere. Real bare bones, trying to keep the bottom line black. But we've got freeze-dried food, gravity showers, and an outhouse."

"We'll settle for a ride home."

"That might take a while. The barge doesn't leave until it's full of the harvest, not for several days."

"Have you got a way for us to call home so people know we're okay?"

"Not this far out. We're just humble subcontractors, so we're on our own. But no worries, we can put you both up until the barge leaves." He turned to Janaina. "Accommodations may be a mite low on amenities."

"It will be better than sleeping in a canoe, no?" Janaina said.

"Indeed it will. We use that third shack as a pantry and for storage. There's room to sling a hammock in there. It's all I got with any privacy."

Walker led them to the third, smaller shack behind the main two. He pushed open the door. It was a single room with shelves full of canned goods and what looked like spare parts. Two screened window openings provided light and a cross-breeze.

"Ain't the Ritz Carlton," Walker said. "Hell, ain't even a Motel Six, but better than bunking with the workers under the thatched roof." He turned to Grant. "Which is where you'll be staying."

Janaina's jaw dropped. "No, that is not necessary. He can stay here as well."

"Oh." Walker looked at Janaina then at Grant with bewilderment. "I didn't realize you two were a couple."

"Actually…" Grant started to say.

Janaina cut him off. "Yes, we have been together quite some time now." She reached over and held Grant's hand.

Grant wondered where this was going.

"Well, I can sling two hammocks in here, but it'll be tight. I bunk in the first building with the office. Marcos, the botanist, is in the one in between us. Y'all come up for dinner at six PM. I'm buying. Unpack and make yourselves at home."

Grant turned both of his pockets inside out. "There. I'm unpacked."

"Traveling light. I like it." Walker smiled and left. Janaina dropped Grant's hand and watched through the pantry window as Walker left.

"I do not trust him," she said.

"He seems okay."

"He is a logger. 'Okay' is not possible."

"Sort of taking a leap there."

"Then why would he lie about having no satellite phone. Everyone out here would have one."

"When you were here on expeditions, did you have one?"

"Well, no. But we were on what you call shoelace budgets."

"That's 'shoestring', and it looks like that's what this place is on. They are just a subcontractor. Give the guy the benefit of the doubt. And by the way, *Janice*, what's with the sudden name change?"

"These men, they are part of Empresa de Madeiras Cruz do Sul. That is a lumber company I fought with a year ago. I exposed their illegal logging, which forced out the CEO and cost them millions in fines. Perhaps these men, they would not recognize my face, especially under all this dirt, but I am very afraid that they might recognize my name."

"And how about you turning us into a couple?"

"I do not wish to stay alone in this shack, the only woman in a camp full of men. But if I say you must stay as a protector, I look weak and afraid, more of a potential victim. If you stay as my boyfriend, that is another thing."

"And I was going to credit my irresistible charm."

"You must be wary. This is a fault you have, this trusting of people. Very American. Very dangerous."

She had a point. She was thinking one step ahead, keeping who they were an unknown, maneuvering to secure a safe place to live. In a million to one shot, he'd come across an American in the middle of the Amazon and thought he was home free. He was so happy to be a step closer to civilization that he'd defaulted to taking everyone at face value.

He shouldn't forget that there were two-legged dangers in the Amazon along with the piranhas and jaguars.

CHAPTER FIVE

A lukewarm gravity shower and scrubbing with industrial-grade soap made Grant feel like a new man. It was a tribute to how far down the civilization ladder he had tumbled. Putting his tattered, dirty clothes back on dampened his elation. He headed back to his pantry bungalow.

Janaina was waiting. She'd taken the first shower as he stood guard. The loggers had been curious, but no one had come over to get friendly. He pretended it was because he'd looked so intimidating. Grant thought she looked cleaner than he did, and realized she'd scrubbed her clothes in the shower. They'd dried quickly in the heat. He'd use that trick tomorrow.

"Ready for a night on the town?" he asked. "First date as a fake couple."

"Ready to eat something," she said. "Anything at this point."

"I'm holding you to that when you are offered freeze-dried kale and sardines."

They headed over to Walker's building. He met them on the porch and welcomed them in.

The main room was the logging office, with two metal desks against the wall. A bunch of official permits from the Brazilian government hung over one of the desks. Cheap folding chairs surrounded a long portable table in the center of the room. Four forks sat atop a stack of plastic plates and an old ceramic tile lay beside them. A metal can at the table's center held two orchids that made the room smell amazing.

"Haven't got any Sunday china and linen to welcome y'all," Walker said. "Kinda barebones operation, you know?"

He stepped into an adjacent room that Grant assumed was his bedroom and returned with a square bottle of American whiskey and a stack of four tiny paper cups.

"But I can offer you a little taste of the USA, distilled down the road from my Kentucky homestead. Saving it for the night we wrap this operation up, but this seems like a good excuse to tap into it early."

Grant looked at Janaina. She shook her head. "Thank you, but I do not drink."

Grant was about to take Walker up on his offer, but remembered he was the only one who had Janaina's back in an isolated compound with twelve strange men. He waved off the whiskey.

"You know, the state I'm in, it would probably put me to sleep in an instant. How about a rain check until the night we leave."

"Suit yourself," Walker said. He poured himself a cup. "As long as I dug the bottle out, I ought to have one, just to make sure it hasn't gone sour or something."

"How does someone from Kentucky end up in the Amazon wilderness?" Grant said.

Walker downed the whiskey in a gulp. "I watched my family work in coal mines and decided that I preferred living in the light of day. Any other work was scarce, so I hitched a few rides to the Pacific Northwest and signed on as a lumberjack. The work suited me, the boss liked me, and I moved up in the organization. Soon I was running my own crew."

He took a seat at the table. Grant and Janaina joined him.

"Then I heard about Cruz do Sul looking for contractors, and paying good, especially if a crew delivered. Figured it was time to be my own boss. Recruited my botanist before I left the States, gathered me a crew when I arrived, and here we are."

The door opened and Gabriel entered carrying a large covered pot. The star on the thick chain slapped against his neck as he tried to balance the heavy pot. He noticed Grant and Janaina and shrank away from the table.

"Don't worry, son," Walker said. "These folks are fine. Just dropped in for a visit. You can put that on the table there."

Gabriel practically tip-toed to the table and placed the pot on the ceramic tile like it was made of antique porcelain. He stepped back and gave Janaina a blushing, sideways glance. She smiled at him and he headed out the door.

"Looks like competition on the horizon, Professor," Walker said. "I need to tell that boy you are spoken for, miss."

"He's the cook?" Grant said.

"Well, he *can* cook, which is more than I can say for any of the others. Came in with his brother, who works enough for two, which is good because Gabriel works for less than one. Between the two of 'em,

I'm still ahead. Gabriel ain't screwed together quite right, but he's simple harmless, not simple scary."

Walker opened the lid of the pot. Pink chunks of meat protruded from a pile of white rice. Pungent seasonings drifted into the air on the escaping steam.

"Really just Spam and rice," Walker said. "But some mix of local spices makes it taste much better than that sounds."

The door opened again. In stepped a younger Hispanic man late 20s, slightly built, wearing round, thick-rimmed glasses. He stopped and gave Grant and Janaina a suspicious appraisal.

"And this is Javier Marcos, our botanist," Walker said.

"Forest assassin," Janaina said under her breath.

Grant shot her an admonishing look. She replied with feigned innocence. He stood up to greet Marcos.

"Dr. Grant Coleman," he said.

"A pleasure to meet you, Dr. Coleman." Marcos didn't look Grant straight in the eyes. His weak handshake gave Grant a little shiver.

"And this is Janice Tucker," Walker continued, "his assistant."

Janaina rose and offered her hand with the enthusiasm of an inmate heading to Death Row. Marcos gave her the same washed out greeting.

Marcos raised an eyebrow as they shook hands. "Have we met? You seem familiar."

Fear flashed across Janaina's face, then she hid it. "No, but I get that all the time."

Grant needed to change the subject before Marcos blew Janaina's cover story. He clamped the little man on the shoulder and startled him. "You haven't an accent to your English. Are you American as well?"

"No, I've traveled there a bit, but I'm Mexican, studied at the university in Sinoloa, Mexico."

"We're here because we're lost. What's your excuse?"

"That's my fault," Walker said. "I had a botanist lined up for the trip and he cancelled at the last minute, but he left Javier's name as a recommended replacement. He was kind enough to join us in this little slice of paradise."

A bug bit Grant's neck. He slapped it.

Marcos turned back to Janaina with narrowed eyes. "Your accent says that you are Brazilian."

"I'm Dr. Coleman's interpreter for local and indigenous people."

Now Marcos' eyes lit up. "You've worked with the local tribes?"

"A little bit."

"Do they have any stories, any myths about the area?"

"Such as…?"

"Stories from before colonization. From times of the Aztecs?"

Walker looked irritated. "Javier, I don't think these people are interested."

"You think Aztecs settled this far south?" Janaina said.

"I've done a lot of research that says they did."

"Honestly, my group is much more interested in avoiding the tribes rather than quizzing them. We think the best way to protect their lives is to not get involved in them."

Her sharp response seemed to sever his enthusiasm. "I see. Of course."

"Enough shop talk," Walker said. "This is a social occasion." He picked up a paper cup and the whiskey bottle. "Javier, let me hit you with a shot of this."

Marcos took him up on the offer. All four sat down to dinner.

As Walker promised, the dinner was far greater than the sum of its parts, or else Grant was so hungry he'd eat anything. After a plate of food, Marcos rose from the table.

"I'm afraid that I have an early morning tomorrow," Marcos said. "I need to scout our next stand of mahogany."

Grant saw an opportunity for he and Janaina to also make a gracious exit. "And speaking for both of us, we're beat. A comfortable night's sleep is way overdue."

"I've offered what limited hospitality I can," Walker said with a smile. "I can do no more. Good night to y'all. Javier, before you go, show me on the map what you've scouted today."

Janaina led Grant out the door and toward their cabin. Once out of earshot of Walker's office, she turned to Grant with an angry look. "Legal or not, felling the forest does not sit well with me."

"You know what doesn't sit well with *me*? Marcos. Am I the only one getting a creepy vibe from him?"

"Oh no, he is a strange little man. A little obsessed with the Aztec history, no?" Janaina said. "And credentials from Sinoloa are no gateway to a job with a Brazilian company. We have more qualified people from our own universities. That part of Mexico is practically run by drug cartels, no?"

"Oh, yes," Grant said. "But Walker is a private contractor. Beggars can't be choosers, especially with a last minute opening."

Janaina shook her head. "See, you are doing that trusting thing again."

"I trust you."

"That is because you are wise. You trust others because you are foolish."

"I can't be wise and foolish at the same time."

"Somehow you manage it."

CHAPTER SIX

The next morning, Grant sat on the front stoop of their building to give Janaina a little private space for getting clean and dressed. He inspected a pack of freeze-dried something. The label on the outside wasn't in English. He ripped it open. Looking inside did not aid in the identification process. The tan colored block could have as easily been hash browns, some kind of meat, or Styrofoam packing material. He took a bite out of it. Based on the flavor, the Styrofoam option went to the top of the list.

"You can put water with that," Janaina said from behind him.

"I considered it. But I'd add effort without adding edibility, so I skipped the step. First thing when we get back in the world I'm eating a triple cheeseburger. Hey, we're in a jungle, right? Aren't there bananas and stuff growing around?"

"Oh we can eat native if you wish. We can dig up some roots, maybe a few grubs." She plucked an ant from the edge of the porch and held it in front of Grant. "And the jungle is full of protein."

Grant chewed the dehydrated block and offered a fake smile. "Uh, you know, this stuff is starting to grow on me."

Walker stepped up to the porch.

"Got something up your alley," he said. "Y'all want to take a peek at a demon?"

"I don't get it," Grant said.

Walker smiled. "The crew dropped a tree at the western edge of the site yesterday. The roots pulled up and exposed some kind of a fossil. The crew thinks it's a demon. Lucky for me, a pair of professionals dropped in to set them straight. Y'all up for it?"

Grant felt the familiar surge of excitement a paleontological discovery always spawned. "You bet I am!"

"*We* are," Janaina corrected.

Grant had forgotten that she was supposed to be his assistant. "Yes, we, certainly. Team effort. Let's go."

Grant and Janaina followed Walker across the clear cut. Along a slope at the western edge, one huge mahogany tree lay on its side, roots ripped out of the ground. A few men stood well away from the tree. The rest lounged in the sleeping area. Walker stopped beside the crown. The nearby men retreated.

"Rains had loosened up the soil. Damn tree toppled over before we even finished cutting it." Walker headed down to the roots.

Janaina turned to Grant, face red with fury.

"That shows how thin the soil is here," she whispered, "and why they should not be logging at all."

"But they have the permits to legally do it," Grant whispered back. "Like it or not. Let's just stay friends with everyone and get a ride downriver."

Grant and Janaina followed Walker to the uprooted base of the tree. An uneven sandstone surface lay exposed. Grant sucked in a deep breath.

The fossilized bones of a giant snake protruded from the stone. The skull and a dozen ribs stood out in near perfect articulation. Thirty-centimeter fangs threatened from a skull a meter and a half long.

"Behold the demon," Walker said with derision.

"That cannot be real," Janaina said.

"It certainly can," Grant said. "About fifty-eight million years ago, the Titanoboa ruled this area. It grew to a length of almost thirteen meters."

"That is what this is?"

"No, the boa has a different shaped head. See the curve of this head, the shape of the fangs, the faint outline of raised scales like eyelashes? This is closer to a pit viper. The boa lives near the water, kills by constriction. This was terrestrial, killed with venom. You did not screw with this snake."

"Well, it won't be killing anybody now." Walker turned to look at a few workers standing near the covered sleep area at the clear cut's far edge. "I need to get these people back to work."

"You should preserve this fossil," Grant said. "It has great scientific value."

"The trees have great financial value, professor."

Grant tried a different tack. "So does this. A lot of expeditions would pay to excavate it. Pay you, not the lumber company. As soon as we get back to civilization, I can tell the right people."

Walker scratched his chin. He looked around the clearing. "We could move a touch more south. I'll set this area aside." He pointed at the uprooted tree. "But after we harvest that."

"You won't regret it," Grant said.

Walker left the two of them and headed over to an idle group of workers.

"It looks like this could have swallowed a man whole," Janaina said.

"If man had been around fifty-eight million years ago. But these creatures are long gone." He bent and traced a finger along a fang. "And that's a hell of a good thing."

CHAPTER SEVEN

Hours later and kilometers farther into the jungle, Marcos swung his machete and slashed away palm fronds that blocked his way. He kicked them aside and revealed the bare, hard-packed earth beneath. He knelt and probed the dirt with the tip of the blade. It struck stone. He flipped the earth aside.

Chiseled, grey stone lay exposed to daylight for the first time in centuries. Marcos ran his fingers along the glossy surface, polished smooth by a million footfalls over the ages. He broke into a smile.

The satellite imaging had hinted that this discovery awaited him. It had not lied. Cruz do Sul had handed Walker the imagery to search out the hardwoods for harvest. Marcos did that, but he could see more. Unnatural shifts in slope and elevation, changes in the IR spectrum. The clues indicated that hundreds of years ago, this jungle had been tamed. Now he had his first proof.

The capstones of a finished road lay before him. The Aztec had come this far into the Amazon, and in high numbers if it warranted the labor to construct this pull cart highway. If his theory was correct, his prize lay to the west.

He followed the buried roadway. Animals and the indigenous had continued to use it and though covered with earth, the traveled section in the center remained free from the encroaching jungle. With each step his anticipation grew. His search was about to yield the treasure he'd dreamed of.

A few kilometers down the path, a sweet floral scent overwhelmed him. It filled the air and grew stronger as he advanced.

The trail opened into a clearing. Ahead rose a dense wall of trees, separated from the jungle by an open strip of calf-high grass. The trees ran in an arc in both directions. Orchids covered every branch. He'd never seen so many flowers in one place. The barrier rose like a fragrant, beautiful fortress.

He approached the wall in awe. This was no natural growth. The trees had been planted, the orchids tended, for generations before they both could maintain this kind of pattern on their own. And from the height of the trees, they'd been growing for centuries. And the line of trees did not parallel the road, they cut across it. These weren't plantings to complement the highway. They were made to block it.

Where the orchid wall crossed the road, a large stone lay half-concealed in the grass. Marcos knelt beside it and pulled away the grass. It was a stela, two meters tall when it had once stood erect. Moss and black mold coated Aztec hieroglyphs along the sides. Marcos had to stifle a scream of joy. This proof of Aztec habitation was incontrovertible.

But was it proof of what he was looking for?

He raked the machete blade across the stela's surface. Layers of living encrustation flew away. The blade chipped away sections of the crumbling stone beneath. He ran a finger along the carvings and stopped at the glyph he'd dreamed of finding. A stylized snake overlaid upon an outline of the sun. The signature of the Viper King.

The stories his Brazilian grandfather had told of the lost city of the rich Viper King, were true.

Excitement washed away caution. He scraped the rest of the stela clean and dashed off a quick translation of the exposed symbols. A story of war and bloodshed. A wall built to entomb the Viper King and his evil demons. A warning that death awaits those who breach the wall and release the...

He struggled with the odd, combination glyph.

Crawling reapers?

Whatever that was supposed to mean, it was a moot point now. Anyone the victorious Aztec King had trapped on the other side of this wall had died centuries ago. And threats of demons might terrify the superstitious workers at the camp, but to a man firmly living in the 21st century, they inspired no fear.

What would be on the other side of this wall would be the capital city of the Viper King, and the legendary temple he'd built to honor himself, and then filled with the treasures of his vanquished foes to sustain him in the afterlife.

Marcos had worked for the Sinoloa drug cartel since he was sixteen, making deliveries, driving the death squads, tending fields in their secret American farms. Still he lived day-to-day, worried about the risk without sharing the riches. He knew he'd never be intimidating enough to rise up and own a hacienda filled with beautiful women. But now, after he stripped the pyramid beyond this wall, he'd live like more of a king than any of them. All his research, and his murder of this expedition's botanist in order to take his place, would all be worth it.

It was late in the day and such a discovery should be addressed in the morning, with a full day ahead of him. But he could not wait. What was to keep one of the workers from wandering through the jungle and discovering the site? He'd tell everyone, and once Cruz do Sul caught wind of this discovery, the riches within would permanently slip through Marcos' fingers.

He had to claim his prize now.

He raised his machete over his head and charged at the orchid wall. He slashed at the thicket of branches, chopping without plan or reason, except to open a hole for himself through the barrier. Orchid nectar coated his blade and splattered his shirt as he chopped at the flowers and the branches that hosted them.

As the branches fell away, he noticed that the tree to his right was dead, the trunk rotted through. The branches of the trees beside it had grown around it. This was the chink in the armor erected by the Aztec King. Topple this dead tree, and it would take down a gap big enough to drive a truck through.

He chopped away at the rotten trunk. Chunks of wood flew through the air and exposed a soggy, hollow core. Nature had already fought half this battle for him. Marcos smiled. He laid the machete blade into the tree with renewed gusto.

Wood creaked, then cracked. Marcos ran back a few steps.

The tree began to lean away from him. Then in a slow-motion acceleration, it gathered speed. The trunk snapped with a sound like a rifle shot and the tree plummeted to the ground. Its great weight pulled the surrounding branches down with it. They sheared off and orchid leaves exploded into the air like the world's sweetest smelling snowstorm. The mass of trees and flowers hit the ground with a crash. Animals in the jungle squawked in surprise.

When the chaos settled and silence returned, the Aztec wall had a six meter breech. On the other side, the ground around the wall was also cleared, covered only in the same tall grasses. The old highway stones were more visible and their path disappeared into the jungle.

Marcos ran through the gap. Orchid petals stuck from his hair and plastered his shirt, but there was no time to get tidy when riches awaited. He stopped on the other side of the wall.

The grass here was taller, nearly waist-high except for on the paved road. Ahead, the jungle canopy covered the path and created the illusion of a tunnel into an abyss. Flickers of dread sparked to life in his chest.

To the left, something in the jungle moved. Something big. He was about to rationalize that it was the wind when the same noise came from off to his right. Then they sounded again in stereo.

Whatever was out there had him outnumbered and it sounded like each had him out-sized. He couldn't live a life of leisure if he was too dead to live it. He took one slow backward step and ducked down below the tops of the grass.

Branches and bushes snapped from along the jungle's edge. Creatures growled in a gravelly rumble. Whatever was out there charged. The sound of branches hitting branches was replaced by the whoosh of flattening grass. The creatures were coming for him.

He had no time to run. He scrambled back into the mass of broken branches and obliterated orchids from the fallen tree. He buried himself under the leaves and closed his eyes, unwilling to watch his last few terrifying moments on earth. Feeling them would be enough.

Two creatures scrambled by, heavy things from the sounds of their footfalls. Were there two, three, four? So much noise, so hard to tell. His heart beat so hard that he was certain it would call the creatures right to him.

But it did not. The animals moved through the opening and into the jungle beyond. He hadn't gotten a look at them.

He stood and checked the grasses. Wide paths had been crushed flat. Whatever beasts had passed were too big to be jaguars, or any other Amazonian predator. Perhaps they'd been tapirs, trapped in the fortress that surrounded the Viper King's domain. He'd let himself be terrorized by a relatively harmless creature. After a long, hard, hot day, his imagination had gotten the best of him.

As the adrenaline washed away, he felt unbelievably weak. He checked his watch. It was late. Perhaps this *could* wait for tomorrow. He'd give whatever else had been trapped within these walls the chance to escape to the rest of the world overnight. Then tomorrow morning, he'd be here before dawn to see what treasures he'd discovered.

He passed back through the breach in the wall. Several trails in the grass led to the jungle beyond. He angled away from those paths and followed the old Aztec road back to camp.

He kept his machete out and ready.

CHAPTER EIGHT

Grant and Janaina's day had been as close to relaxing as they'd had in weeks. While the loggers had finally overcome their fear of the "stone demon" and gotten back to work, the two of them had nothing to do but wait for the ride downriver. Only when Grant felt the relative safety of the camp did he realize how hyper-alert he'd been for so long. It was like a weight off his shoulders.

He could tell Janaina didn't feel quite the same. Her dislike of the tree harvest and her fear of being exposed as a past scourge of Cruz do Sul seemed to keep her on edge all day.

Their dinner invitation had apparently been a one-time thing, as Walker hadn't asked them over that night. Grant didn't see Marcos all day, and that was fine with him. The weasely guy gave him the creeps.

That night, Grant and Janaina fell asleep almost as the sun set. But after a few hours, Grant woke up. He looked across the room to see the shadow of Janaina sitting up in her hammock. He reached over and clicked on the cheap electric lantern that hung from the wall. In the weak light, Janaina looked very sad.

"What are you doing awake?" he asked.

"I could not stay asleep. I tried how you say, counting ships, but it did not help."

"It's counting sheep. Something bothering you?"

"Only everything. Where we are, who we are with, what they are doing."

"This is very temporary. We'll be home soon. And for now we're safe."

From outside sounded a crash so loud that it shook the building.

"What the hell?" Grant jumped from his hammock and pulled open the front door.

The moon had yet to rise. The darkness outside was near absolute. A few lamps flared to life in the worker's area. Down by the river, metal scraped against earth.

"Even though this is what everyone who dies in a horror movie says," Grant said. "I'd better go check on that."

"You fear there are dangerous animals out there in the daytime? Nighttime is twice as worse."

"Those sounds came from where the barge is tied up. I don't want anything happening to our ride home."

"Then I am going with you."

"This is where I'm supposed to tell you to stay back because it isn't safe, right?"

"You are correct. Are you going to?"

"I'm guessing it wouldn't matter."

"And you are correct again."

He handed her a second lantern. "Then off we go."

She followed him out the door. The electric lantern did a poor job of lighting anything more than a few meters away. To the right, several lanterns coming from the worker's area bobbed in the darkness ahead of them. To the left, the boss's shack remained dark.

"Chad Walker is one sound sleeper," Grant said.

They continued down to the river. The workers' lanterns lit the river's edge like a string of Christmas lights. The barge rocked, still anchored to the riverbank. Nervous voices twittered in Spanish and Portuguese from the shadows.

At the far end of the group, a man screamed. His lantern flew up in the air, hit the ground with the smash of broken glass, and went dark. The man screamed again, from higher up. The scream turned to a wail, and then went silent.

Suddenly, the barge lifted straight up out of the water, nearly exposing the keel. The men along the river shouted warnings and sprinted away from the river. The barge tipped toward the shore. Chains snapped and a dozen logs tumbled out after the men like giant pick-up sticks. One log bounced and landed on a worker, pounding him into the dirt.

Then the barge flipped upside down, and slammed onto the shoreline just feet away. Mud exploded from the impact and splattered Grant and Janaina. Something skittered beneath the trees. Many of the workers ran back to their hammocks.

Everything went quiet.

"Are you okay?" Grant said.

"Yes. You?"

Grant scraped mud from his arms. "Nothing a hot shower couldn't fix. If we had one."

They hurried to the man crushed by the rolling log. Only the lower half of his legs stuck out from under the log. They didn't move.

"Damn," Grant whispered.

They stepped over to the inverted barge. The impact had put a fold in the hull and a tear along the underside. Even if they could use some sort of logging equipment to flip the thing back over, it would never float again.

Two of the workers who hadn't fled inspected the barge by the light of their lamp. They chattered in excited, terrified Portuguese. Janaina stepped over and asked a few questions. One of the men responded with rapid-fire Portuguese, wide eyes, and broad sweeps of his lantern.

"What did he say?" Grant asked.

Janaina shook her head. "*O demônio*. They are convinced it is the work of the demon whose bones were under that tree. It has come to destroy them for disturbing its sleep."

"He can't be serious."

"There are many myths of giant creatures in the Amazon."

"Probably inspired by fossilized discoveries like we saw today."

"Do I hear doubt about giant animals from a man who killed an ankylosaur a few days ago?"

"That was on a plateau isolated from the world for thousands of years. This place isn't so remote that it can hide animals that big."

"Fine. Then what is it that turned our big boat upside down?"

"Natural gas," said Walker from behind them.

He stepped up next to the barge and ran his lantern along the hull. "The place is ripe with natural gas pockets. Too dirty and too intermittent to rate recovery. But every now and then a pocket of it works its way to the surface, especially through soft river sediments. I've seen bubbles big enough to flip this boat over."

Grant was more than ready to accept that plausible explanation. "Makes more sense than a rampaging demon."

"All these people need to get back to their bunks." Walker marched over to the remaining workers and gave them some angry orders in Portuguese. They gave the overturned boat a wary look, then backed away toward the workers' quarters, talking to each other in hushed tones. Walker returned.

"This is gonna turn the schedule into a damn goat rope," Walker said. "The boat's towing us up an empty barge, and now we'll need to spend a day loading that instead of just swapping barges. And this wreck will be a company loss. They'll be mighty pissed."

As long as they were still coming, and he and Janaina were still hitching a downriver ride, Grant wasn't going to be as upset as Walker about this. Random natural gas eruptions were just another reason to get the hell out of the Amazon as fast as possible.

CHAPTER NINE

There was still time before dawn. Emiliano stared up at the thatched roof of the workers' sleep area. After the demon had flipped the barge at the river, he hadn't been back to sleep.

Beside him, two hammocks hung empty.

He knew it was now or never. The demon spirit was awakened. Next time it returned, it would do worse. They were lucky only one man had been killed and one gone missing. He and Gabriel weren't going to be next.

He slipped out to his feet and pulled on his torn T-shirt. Snoring reverberated between the hammocks.

Emiliano crept to his younger brother Gabriel's hammock. Gabriel lay with his arms wrapped around his shoulders, the same way he'd slept when he'd rocked himself to sleep as a child. Emiliano nudged him. Gabriel's eyes opened to slits.

"Emiliano?" Gabriel mumbled.

"Shh, come with me. Don't wake the others." He knew Gabriel would follow with no more details than that.

He led Gabriel out from under the roof and across the clearing they'd helped cut in the jungle. Insects buzzed from all sides. The half moon provided just enough light to step around the larger obstacles. They stopped at the clearing's edge.

"We can't stay here," Emiliano said.

He couldn't read his younger brother's face in the pre-dawn darkness. But as always, he could sense the spike in his fear.

"Where would we go?" Gabriel said.

The big brother responsibility had always rested on Emiliano's shoulders, and it weighed a bit heavier than for most, since Gabriel had always been so much slower than the other boys. Emiliano had always been the one who had a plan.

Except for now.

"Away," Emiliano said. "Anywhere."

He wasn't certain what had attacked the camp last night. But whatever it was, it was nothing he wanted to tangle with. A demon was as good an explanation as any, and one he could get Gabriel to understand.

"You saw what the men uncovered today," he said. "You saw what happened to the barge. The demon is loose."

"The boss man said the barge wasn't destroyed by a demon. He said it was some kind of gas bubble."

"You are going to believe his lies? You saw Ricardo snatched from the ground. Did a gas bubble do that?"

"Well..." Gabriel wound the tail of his shirt around his right hand, the tell-tale sign of terror that Gabriel had displayed since he was three. "...if it is a demon, it will kill us here, it will kill us there. Better to be here with others."

"No, the others will feed its blood lust. We'll get far away from its bones, away from the space it defends. We'll cut through the jungle to a place downstream, make a raft like we said we'd do when we were kids. Remember that?"

Gabriel smiled a little. "I remember. Our big adventure."

"Yes, we'll finally have the big adventure. We'll get downriver and hitch a ride to the coast."

Gabriel turned away. The moonlight lit his broad face and showed his eyes consumed by dread.

Always the same. A brother two years younger, but inches taller. Emiliano always having to coax the bigger, stronger Gabriel into anything outside of his narrow experience. Persuading him to join this logging crew had been a Herculean task. Now just when he'd adapted to this life, even distinguished himself by doing cooking for the boss, Emiliano had to convince him to overturn it. But if he didn't, he was certain they'd both end up dead. He reached over and grabbed the star that hung on a chain around Gabriel's neck.

"You remember when I made this for you? When you were little?"

"Yes."

"I said it would remind you that I was always there to guide you, like the Bethlehem star, and keep you safe. Haven't I done that?"

Gabriel reluctantly nodded.

"If we stay here," Emiliano said, "we'll end up like Ricardo or Jose. One by one the demon will take us down. Haven't I always made sure you were safe?"

"Uh, yes. I guess."

"Then let me make you safe now. Make us both safe. I have enough food in my pack for both of us for a few days. We have to go now."

Gabriel looked back at the hammocks swinging under the open thatched roof. Then down at the upended barge along the river. Then into Emiliano's eyes.

"Okay. We'll go do the adventure."

Emiliano reached up and clapped his brother on the shoulder. "Alright then. We're off."

***

Forty minutes later, as the rising sun lit the jungle into its full emerald brilliance, Emiliano realized how daunting the journey ahead would be. He really did not know how far away the bend in the river was, just that a map he'd seen said it was there. He didn't know if an impenetrable swamp lay ahead, or what predators might be lurking in the shadows. But while death was possible up ahead, it was certain at the camp they'd left behind.

Gabriel hadn't said a word since they'd departed. He hadn't asked how much longer it would take, hadn't complained about breaking trail, hadn't asked for food or water. It was as if once he'd agreed to Emiliano's plan, he'd entrusted Emiliano to make it all happen. That only made Emiliano's burden feel even heavier.

A puff of air swirled through the trees and brought with it an intoxicating, floral scent. It was like a flower vendor through an amplifier.

The jungle opened to a clearing. Ahead across a sea of tall grass stood a wall of orchids that seemed to grow among a stand of trees. Part of it had fallen in and created a gap in the wall. A beaten path through the grasses led to the opening. That meant that others had traveled this way. Which meant that finally, in this trackless jungle, they'd found a hint of civilization.

"Gabriel, this is the way."

He stepped out into the clearing. Gabriel grabbed his arm and held him back.

"Emi, this looks scary."

Emiliano jerked his arm free of his brother's grasp. There were times Gabriel's disability could be so frustrating. Would he rather they stay in the jungle with jaguars, or swim the river with the piranhas? "Gabi, it's fine. Stop being a baby."

Gabriel looked hurt, and Emiliano immediately regretted his choice of words. But with no time to spare, his brother might need to manage a few hurt feelings. He headed down the track of trodden grass toward the opening in the wall. Gabriel hesitated, then followed.

Halfway to the opening they came across a stone stela lying on the ground. Emiliano bent and pulled away the grass that covered the symbols. They looked like the ones he'd seen in movies about the Aztec Kings. Several of them contained carvings of a huge snake.

Gabriel yelped. "Ai, see? It's the demon from the ground. This is a warning. This is its home."

"Gabi, that's nonsense. These are hundreds of years old. They mean nothing."

Something moved in the jungle on the other side of the orchid wall. Something huge.

Emiliano's heart skipped a beat. He jumped to his feet.

Gabriel trembled, staring wide-eyed at the gap in the wall. "I told you!"

Palm fronds closer to the gap swayed. Branches snapped.

Emiliano didn't need his curiosity satisfied about what was about to come through that opening. He grabbed his brother's shirt and pulled. "Run!"

They both turned and retreated down the trail through the grass. At the clearing's edge, they plunged back into the jungle. Branches reached out to slow their escape. The two blindly slashed at them with their machetes, always running. Branches tore at their clothes and scraped their skin.

Behind them, sounded a growl like a lion with a higher pitch. Stems snapped and leaves shredded as the creature closed on them. Panic ripped through Emiliano.

But it gripped Gabriel harder. He swerved right, breaking a new trail through the jungle. Emiliano didn't have the breath to call to him, or even the time to look back. Whatever had burst out from behind the orchid wall was so close that he could smell it, a stink like dead armadillo and dirty fur.

A root caught his leg. He dropped and hit the earth hard. The growling sounded right above him and hot breath blew against his neck. He rolled over and faced two pitch black eyes in a furry face. Huge hairy legs straddled him on both sides. It was a spider the size of a car.

Two mandibles spread open and the creature tore into his shoulder.

He screamed. The pain made the world turn white.

His last thought before it all went dark was a prayer that his brother had escaped.

CHAPTER TEN

The sun blazing through the window pulled Marcos from his sleep. He opened an eye and cursed. The unaccustomed physical exertion of chopping through the jungle had taken more out of him than he'd realized. The earplugs he used to drown out the insect drone of the jungle night had also blocked the noise of the awakened camp. He pulled them out and rolled out of his hammock. Sore muscles screamed at him in response.

He checked his watch. He was two hours behind schedule. It wasn't like the undiscovered pyramid was going anywhere, but it would take time to get to the thing and then find a way inside. He'd hoped to do both in one day.

He got dressed and threw some supplies, food, and water into a backpack. He tucked his machete into his belt and took a shovel from the corner of the room. He really hoped that he wouldn't have to use either.

He peered out the window. A lot of men labored down by the barge, likely re-stacking timber. That would be a good distraction. He could tell anyone he was heading out to check the area for new hardwoods and they would not stop him, but dealing with the tedium of lying wasn't on his agenda. He was ready to get rich, courtesy of the Viper King.

Marcos darted out the door and into the jungle. He returned to the trail he'd cut along the old Aztec roadway the day before and headed for the orchid wall.

CHAPTER ELEVEN

Grant and Janaina hadn't slept well. After the disaster on the river, between the adrenaline and the dread of the unknown, they only managed a few interrupted hours, and none of them simultaneous. Grant welcomed dawn's arrival. Janaina set out after sunrise, as if dying to relieve some claustrophobia. Grant stepped out about an hour later. He met Walker as soon as he left the building.

"Two more damn men took off," Walker said. "The beached barge sent the demon myth sailing over the moon. Kind of surprised only two ran away."

"To where?" Grant said.

"If they decided to take their chances in the jungle, they'll settle for anywhere. I've seen people tie a few logs together and try to raft downstream. Sort of works until you get to a waterfall, or a crocodile decides to share the ride."

"Here's hoping that they make it," Grant said.

"Here's hoping we can still get a full load of timber ready by the time the barge arrives."

Grant wasn't impressed by Walker's lack of concern for his deserted employees.

The two of them continued down to the river to give the barge a closer inspection. Prints marred the sand, though not footprints. They were circular, the size of a saucer, with an indistinct outline. They didn't look like anything Grant had ever seen before.

As the two approached the barge Janaina was already there. She stood by, watching men wrangle the scattered logs into a pile. The poor victim who'd been crushed last night was gone, and, Grant hoped, given a deep and decent burial. He approached Janaina. Walker went to give the barge a closer look.

"I have no faith in this being our ride home," Janaina said.

Grant had to agree. The barge wasn't going to ever float again. The impact had broken the keel.

On a section of the hull by the bow, fresh steel shined in the sunlight. The paint had been stripped from an area a meter wide and twice as long. In the drying mud beneath lay a mound of black paint flecks. Grant gave them a nudge with his boot. They were a solid mass.

"What is that?" Janaina said.

"No idea," Grant said. "Someone scraped something sticky from the hull after the accident last night."

He led Walker and Janaina around the barge. They picked their way through some scattered logs to the stern. Another patch of bare metal glittered from about three meters up, with another pile of paint chips on the ground. This pile had the impression of a boot sole in it. Grant stepped up on a log for a closer look. Faint scrapes marred the steel.

"Someone worked hard to clean something off the hull last night," Grant said.

"Or the steel flexed and paint just fell off," Walker said. "The barges shed paint all the time. It's the damn jungle climate."

Janaina stepped up on the log beside them. She ran a finger across the bare steel.

Several workers shouted at Grant in Portuguese and made motions to shoo him away. He and Janaina stepped off the log and back closer to the clearing's edge. Six men lifted the log and carried it to the growing pile.

A shattered lantern from last night lay on the ground at Janaina's feet. "This was where that man was taken," she said.

Grant scanned the jungle floor. Several smaller branches hung freshly broken. They made a trail into the jungle. "And somewhere out there was where he was taken to."

"A jaguar would do that," Walker said. "Grab prey and then take it elsewhere."

"At the same time the barge explodes out of the river? Kind of a coincidence."

"Not if it was waiting at the clearing's edge for the opportunity to attack. It waits, then there's one confused man alone, it pounces. It's how they hunt herd animals."

"I'm not sure I like how our current herd is being thinned out."

Walker looked back at the men trying to salvage the timber load. "Look at that. They're going to damage that timber even worse." He rushed off to the men, shouting orders in Spanish and Portuguese.

"He might be alive," Janaina said.

"You're not going to suggest…"

"Walker isn't going to pull anyone away from work. We should go see if the missing man is still alive."

He hated to admit she had a point. No one else seemed ready to try. He pointed to the path through the jungle. "Follow the Yellow Brick Road, Dorothy."

Janaina looked at the path, then at him. "It does not look yellow."

"Never mind. It's a quote from an old movie. Follow the trail."

The two set off along the track of crushed greenery. Whatever creature had snatched the worker had snapped enough branches and trampled enough ferns that it had to have been pretty big. Grant realized they were heading into the unknown with no means of defense.

A few minutes later, they stopped dead in their tracks. At their feet, the previous night's victim lay on the ground beside a huge mahogany tree. He looked like he was wrapped in a silvery gauze. His eyes were half-open. Glassy. Dead.

Janaina bit her lip. Grant advanced and knelt beside the man. His gray, sunken skin promised there was no point checking for a pulse. He touched the threads that bound the man. They were coarse and sticky.

"What is that around him?" Janaina said. "It looks like what the ants on the plateau made."

Indeed it did resemble the residue excreted by the giant ants back on the plateau. "No, it's different. Finer. Spun, not spit. More like spider web than anything else."

Palm fronds rustled a few meters away. Grant jumped to his feet. More branches moved.

"I say we get back to camp and come back for this body with reinforcements."

"A wise choice," Janaina said.

They both backed down the trail until the jungle obscured the corpse. Then they turned and bolted the rest of the way to the clearing. They burst out of the jungle and practically ran over Walker.

"Hey, what are you two doing out there?" Walker said. "Damn, you look like you've seen a ghost."

"As close as I want to get," Grant said between rapid breaths. He was really going to get in shape as soon as he got home. "We found your worker's corpse."

Walker looked more concerned than relieved. "Where?"

"A short distance into the jungle. Covered in what looks like spider webs."

"I doubt spiders dragged him off."

"Whatever did, killed him in a bizarre way. I've never seen a body look the way his did."

"Okay, we'll go check it out. Wait here."

Walker jogged back to the office and returned with a hunting rifle. "Okay. Show me where he is."

"Shouldn't we be armed as well?" Grant said.

"I'm armed enough for the three of us, let's just go."

Grant led the three of them back into the jungle. They arrived back at the big mahogany. The body was gone.

"Well?" Walker said.

"It was right here. We both saw it."

Walker relaxed. "He couldn't have been real dead if he walked away."

"He was definitely too dead to do that."

Walker scanned the trees. He stepped forward and pointed up to the canopy with the rifle barrel. "Look up there."

Grant and Janaina moved next to him. A jet-black jaguar lay across one of the upper branches. It stared down at them with fierce, yellow eyes. The worker's corpse hung wedged in the crook beside it.

"Jaguar got him. You two probably startled the kitty when he was taking the body away. As soon as you left, he took it to a safe place in the trees."

The jaguar made a little growl and leapt to an adjoining tree.

"A big cat didn't kill that worker," Grant said. "Felines have killed the same way for ten thousand years. There would have been a massive neck wound."

"And what about all the webbing around the body?" Janaina added.

"Spider webs," Walker said. "Jungle's full of them. Sometimes they're so thick they block a trail. Jaguar just dragged the body through some. Sad that this boy got killed, but it's no mystery how. Simplest explanations, they're usually the right one." He gave the corpse in the tree another appraisal. "No way the jag's going to let us get that body back without killing the cat."

"You cannot shoot it; it is too rare," Janaina said.

"Even if I did, I couldn't convince any of these spooked workers to go up that tree to get it." He laid the rifle back across his shoulder. "We'd better get back to camp."

Walker retreated back down the trail.

"I hate to admit it," Grant said, "but he's right about bringing back the body."

"But wrong about everything else," Janaina said. "Those were no normal spider webs."

"You've got that right. We know what we saw."

CHAPTER TWELVE

In hours, Walker had the work crews back in full swing. The tree trunks from the barge were stacked in a pyramid. Chainsaws buzzed at the clearing's edge. Bow saws sang as they severed smaller limbs.

In an open area, one stout man in a red shirt aimed a backpack flamethrower at a pile of discarded branches. An unlit cigarette dangled from his lips. He let loose a stream of liquid fire and the pile burst into flames. He hooted approval at the conflagration.

Men barked orders and others gave cheeky replies in return. Maybe the crew felt better working than worrying about last night's…whatever last night had been.

Grant and Janaina watched from their pantry porch. She shook her head.

"There is just no stop to this," she said. "People die, and yet the trees still fall."

"Walker is a man with a mission. He doesn't have the load ready on time, he probably goes bankrupt."

"My heart does not break for him."

Grant was going to add that if the operation went broke, none of these poor people got paid, but this wasn't the time to debate sustainable harvesting with Janaina. There probably wasn't ever a time to do that.

"I want to get another look at that fossil," he said.

"Go ahead. I will take a walk around the other side. I do not want to watch this."

Grant nodded in understanding. He grabbed some paper and a pencil from the stash in the pantry and headed over to the fossil.

The workers had felled several other trees around the sandstone discovery, and a maelstrom of roaring chainsaws and flashing blades surrounded the find. Grant picked his way through the activity, answering every angry look from an interrupted logger with a repentant smile. The apologetic tone didn't seem to carry much weight.

He knelt beside the snake fossil and made some etchings, especially around the fang and jaw area. Then he noted the articulation of the vertebrae, the apparent size of the brain cavity. It had been pretty damn big.

Something about this find didn't sit right. Floods from the nearby river could have scoured away centuries of sediment, but over fifty million years of rock would take a lot of scrubbing. He usually only found fossils that old when a river had washed away the side of a hill, not by one stripping away horizontal layers.

He pored over the rest of the fossil. He wished he had his tools, hell, any tools. This was a new species. If he brought this back for some peer review, he'd be the one to name it. And his name would be part of that Latin moniker. *Vipera magna colemani.*

Of course his ex-wife's divorce lawyer would probably demand her name be part of it as well.

Now that he thought of it, the snake was pretty horrific. He might just name it after her for spite. That idea brought a smile to his face.

He noticed something odd around one of the snake's vertebrae. Something very black and very out of place. He took a sharp stone and etched the area around it. It had a straight, chipped edge. He didn't need to see the whole thing to know this was an arrowhead, or if it was large enough, a spear point.

That couldn't be possible. Nothing walking the earth fifty-eight million years ago was chipping spear points. So this fossil wasn't fifty-eight million years old.

Or the spear point had washed in later, added to the fossil record as the river exposed this stone to the world again, the way anachronistic artifacts are mixed in archeological sites all over the world. The obvious, simple explanation.

Earlier, Walker had said the simple explanations were usually the correct ones. Grant thought that nugget of wisdom had been wrong about the jaguar attack. Could it be wrong about this spear point theory as well?

He was letting his imagination, colored by his experiences, get the best of him. Snakes this large couldn't possibly have survived into the modern era.

CHAPTER THIRTEEN

Marcos hurried down the jungle trail, eager to get at the treasures hidden beyond the orchid wall. But a hundred meters along the old Aztec highway, Marcos noticed it had changed. There were fresh cuts that he hadn't made, fewer low hanging branches. Someone else had been here since yesterday evening. From the footprints in the earth, more than one somebody.

He clenched a fist. He should have worked through the night last night. He left an opening in the wall and some idiot worker may have discovered it. He didn't need anyone finding his prize before he did.

A few minutes later, something rustled up ahead on the trail. Marcos caught his breath. Whatever had escaped from behind the orchid wall yesterday was out here somewhere, and he had no desire to meet it. He brought the shovel to his shoulder like a baseball bat and crouched beneath a palm.

One of the workers emerged from the trail's far end. Marcos recognized Gabriel, one of the slower workers, who did some cooking for Walker on occasion. The man looked terrified and exhausted. A green liquid and dirt speckled his face and shirt.

Marcos planted the shovel in the ground and stood to block the trail. Gabriel kept his headlong stagger, as if Marcos' presence didn't register. Just before Gabriel ran into him, Marcos reached up and grabbed Gabriel's shoulders. He gave him a shake.

"Gabriel? What happened to you?"

Gabriel's eyes finally focused on Marcos. "Oh, sir. It was so bad. The monster, it killed him."

"Killed who?"

"Emiliano. He fought, but it was too strong."

"What was too strong?"

"The spider. Big as a car."

Marcos sighed and released him. Gabriel was worse than simple, he was crazy.

"It attacked us," Gabriel continued, "outside the orchid wall."

Marcos perked up. His discovery of the wall did not need to be common knowledge. "What wall?"

"In the jungle. By the big stone. The spider, it was so big. I chopped at it, drew it away. But I couldn't save my brother."

"I'm sure you tried," Marcos said without thinking. His mind was already racing through the scenario that was about to unfold. Once Gabriel returned to camp with this story, Walker would have no choice but to lead a party into the jungle to see what had happened first hand. They'd find the orchid wall, and then whatever lay beyond. All his work would be wasted.

Gabriel pulled away. "I have to get to camp, warn the others."

"Yes, yes. Good idea." Marcos shed his backpack and dropped it at Gabriel's feet. "First, you need some water. Here, in my backpack."

"Yes, thank you sir." Gabriel bent over to open the sack.

Marcos struck like a cobra. He whipped the shovel from the ground and brought the spade down at the base of Gabriel's skull. Gabriel moaned and dropped to all fours. Marcos struck him again and again, each time driving Gabriel lower to the ground. Finally the man collapsed.

An irrational fear that others had witnessed what he'd just done swelled inside him. Marcos shot guilty, nervous glances around the jungle. Nothing but trees. Marcos drove the shovel into the ground. He grabbed Gabriel by the wrist and pulled. The body didn't move. The big man probably weighed over a hundred kilos.

Marcos dug in his heels and strained. Gabriel's body inched forward. Marcos dragged him off the trail and behind some ferns.

Gabriel's eyes flickered open. He looked confused. "What...what are you doing?"

"Damn." Marcos said. He looked back at the shovel on the trail. By the time he got it, Gabriel would be back on his feet and Marcos wouldn't catch him by surprise a second time.

Marcos drew the machete from his belt. He swung at Gabriel. Gabriel raised an arm to block the blow. The blade sliced into his forearm and hit bone.

Gabriel screamed. Blood spurted from the wound. He pulled back his arm and grabbed at the gash to stop the bleeding. A look of confused betrayal crossed his face.

"Why?" he whimpered.

The gushing blood sent Marcos' heart racing. All he could think of was Gabriel somehow running back into camp, wounded and screaming that Marcos had tried to kill him. All the effort to join the group, to deal with the jungle, to find his lost treasure, all would be for nothing. That could not happen.

He raised the machete and blindly hacked away. The pounding of blood in Marcos' ears muffled the dying man's cries. Blow after blow chopped at the defenseless worker. By the time Marcos realized what he'd been doing, all resistance had long ceased. He pulled the blade from Gabriel's corpse and stepped away.

What lay on the ground hardly looked like a man anymore, more like ground meat. Marcos fought back the urge to vomit. He staggered away, back to the trail.

Blood painted the machete's blade a damning bright red. He dropped the blade to the ground and scrubbed it clean with dirt and fallen leaves. Then he saw his hands and forearms were splattered in blood. He rubbed them with the jungle floor as well, until his skin tingled and he was nothing but black from the elbows down.

He'd poisoned the first expedition botanist. Hadn't even seen him die. He'd never killed anyone in person before. He'd seen people killed, transported assassins to and from killings, but he'd never ended a life with his own hands. It had played out much messier than he'd expected.

Marcos raised himself from the ground and returned to the trail. He re-sheathed the machete, shouldered his pack and picked up the shovel.

He'd had no choice, he rationalized. It was the life of one peasant laborer or the riches and lifestyle Marcos had always deserved. What were Gabriel and his brother doing out here last night anyway? Running away from camp? They both got what they deserved.

Marcos thought about Gabriel's brother. Killed by a giant spider? The simpleton had to have been confused, or maybe giant meant tarantula-sized to him. At any rate, it made no difference. There was only one path for Marcos to take now. Forward to unlimited wealth. None of this would matter from his new hacienda outside the city.

A chunk of Gabriel's flesh hung from his shirt sleeve. He flicked it away, and then headed west down the trail.

CHAPTER FOURTEEN

Janaina walked along the clearing's edge, water bottle in hand. She'd been in the clearing's center, near the bonfire that the crazy man with the flamethrower was feeding. She'd wanted a running start to get someplace safer if whatever attacked last night attacked again. But the open space had started to feel exposed. So she walked off her anxiety near the tree line, better to be one step away from a hiding place in the jungle's shadows.

Something shuffled in the bush to her right. Janaina's heart jumped into her throat. She sprang away from the jungle.

Leaves swayed off to the right and left, as if two creatures were beating a quick retreat. Then the foliage went still. Janaina exhaled.

From beneath the undergrowth, a man moaned.

Compassion overwhelmed her fear. Janaina crept forward to the clearing's edge. She pulled aside some palm fronds.

One of the workers lay on the ground, slathered in blood.

Janaina stifled a scream from the shock. Then she dropped down by the man's side and checked for a pulse. He was still alive.

She took a water bottle from her pocket and rinsed his bare chest. The blood had made his injuries seem worse than they were. Other than one slash at his left shoulder, the rest of the wounds were small cuts and scratches. She splashed a bit of water on his face. He stirred. She raised his head and put the bottle to his lips. He drank a few swallows and leaned back. His eyes snapped open.

"Gabriel!" he cried.

She laid her hand on his forehead. "Relax. You are safe now."

He sat up and winced. His right hand shot to clamp the wound at his shoulder. "Damn." He looked into her eyes. "You are the fossil hunter. I'm back at the camp?"

43

"Yes. What is your name?"

"Emiliano."

"What happened to you?"

"My brother and I, we left, escaped this demon place. We were attacked by a spider. A giant spider."

The webbing she'd seen around last night's victim kept Janaina from thinking this poor man crazy. "Where is your brother?"

"He isn't here?"

"I only saw you, lying here."

His eyes danced about, too quickly to focus on anything. "This is all my fault. The Aztec carvings warned us, but I ignored them."

"What carvings?"

"In the stone spike on the ground. Snakes and all kinds of creatures. Even Gabriel knew what they meant."

This wasn't making sense to Janaina. She asked a more basic question. "How did you get here?"

"I...I don't know. The spider attacked. I was separated from Gabriel. The spider was on me...that's all I remember." Emiliano stood up. He staggered, then steadied himself. "Gabriel is still out there. I have to get back to the wall and find him."

Janaina remembered Gabriel, who cooked dinner the other night. Then the rest of what Emiliano said registered. "Wait, what wall?"

"The orchid wall by the stone carvings. The spider came from behind that. I have to go back and find my brother."

"Oh no, you have to get that wound cleaned and bandaged. Your brother could be anywhere out there. You cannot run off into the jungle alone."

Emiliano looked about to protest, then he winced as his shoulder sent another stab of pain through his body. He nodded, and turned for the main office.

The blood that had soaked his chest hadn't touched his back. But there was something on the back of his arms.

"Hold on," Janaina said.

He paused and she looked closer at the back of his arms. White smudges coated his biceps. She ran a finger across one. It had the consistency of oil paint. The tip of her finger came away white.

"What is it?" Emiliano said.

She showed him her finger. "Something white. This was from the spider?"

"Could have been. Everything happened so fast."

Emiliano headed to the office building. Janaina wiped the white substance hard against her pant leg and hoped whatever it was wasn't poisonous. Who knew what giant spiders excreted?

Maybe Grant did. She jogged over to where he knelt by the fossilized snake.

CHAPTER FIFTEEN

Grant bent over and ran a finger along the fangs of the fossilized giant snake.

"Of the two of us," he whispered, "I am so glad you're the one who's dead."

Janaina ran up to him, out of breath.

"What's going on?" Grant asked.

"I just found an injured worker named Emiliano at the edge of the jungle. He and Gabriel, the man that cooked for us, were the two who tried to make their way home. They did not get far. A giant spider stopped them."

Grant looked over at the overturned barge from the previous night's attack. "Oddly, I'm willing to accept that outlandish story without reservation."

"Is that your sarcasm voice now?"

"No, I'm serious. A giant spider makes sense. The marks I saw in the earth by the barge that were not quite footprints. The webbing around the victim we saw in the jungle. The draining of fluids from the corpse. These are all spider-like signs."

Walker joined them. "You just sent an injured man into the office?"

"Yes," Janaina said. "I found him in the jungle."

"He was babbling about giant spiders and a wall of flowers," Walker said. "Was his brother with him?"

"No he was alone."

"Great. Well, they were the two who ran off this morning. That crazy story about giant spiders will spread through camp like a plague. Cutting's gonna stop on a dime."

"Hard to believe that spiders the size of a garage would keep people away from cutting down trees," Grant said.

"Now *that* is your sarcasm voice," Janaina said.

Grant smiled at her. "See, you're catching on." He turned back to Walker. "Where's Marcos?"

"Haven't seen him. He was going to do location scouting this morning."

"After last night," Janaina said, "I would not scout anywhere past the edge of the clearing."

"Based on finding a bloody man at the clearing's edge," Grant said, "even that might be pushing it."

"I'm not gonna to sit here and wait for another attack," Walker said. "We're going on a spider hunt."

"By *we*," Grant said, "I hope you're meaning *you*. Right?"

"Hell, no. I'm taking the men into the jungle. We're going to find nothing, or we're going to find something, and then kill the damn thing. Either way we end up back here and then get back to work."

"Or giant spiders kill you all and this place becomes a ghost town."

"Not gonna happen. You coming?"

"Me, no. I've already got a full schedule. Deep muscle massage at eleven. Having my hair done at one. I don't think I could work in a suicidal jungle trek."

"We should go," Janina said.

Grant gave her a double take. "Are you crazy?"

"It is safer surrounded by an armed party than to sit in this defenseless camp."

"And it's safer to book passage on the *Titanic* than either of those options."

"You want to get rid of hornets," Walker said, "then you gotta destroy the nest."

"And Emiliano said there was an Aztec marker outside a broken wall," Janaina said. "That could be a clue to where these things came from and how to get rid of them."

In Grant's struggle to make a decision, reason was beginning to triumph over self-preservation. He reminded himself that kind of thinking had gotten him into mortal combat with giant bats and dinosaurs in the past.

"If we're going to go," he said, "we'll need to be able to read that Aztec marker."

"Not like we got access to Google Translate out here," Walker said.

"I think we can get the next best thing."

Grant led the three of them to Marcos' quarters.

"What are you doing?" Walker said.

"Marcos has an Aztec obsession. He's got to have some references on them in here somewhere."

"You can't just rifle through the man's gear."

"I'll be gentle."

Grant opened the door. The room was empty. Marcos' tastes appeared simple. A sagging bed hugged one wall, a desk nestled into the opposite corner. The single shelf sagged under the weight of stacks of books. He and Janaina began to scan the book spines.

Grant found one on the Aztec language. "Bingo."

He pulled it off the shelf and opened it up on Marcos' desk. There was a huge appendix of hieroglyphs and their English translations.

"There are no botany reference books here," Janaina said, still checking the shelf.

"And?" Walker said.

"And he is a botanist. That is like a carpenter not having a measurement tape."

"Maybe he knows the local plants. Really, I just care about him finding the mahogany."

"This land is filled with undiscovered species. The idea of finding the unfound would be exciting to a botanist. You need a reference book to know if the species has already been identified."

"Maybe all he cares about is finding the mahogany. That *is* what I pay him for."

Grant tucked the Aztec book under his arm. "I'll bring this. With some luck, we'll see what the carvings have to say to us."

"It would be better if Marcos was part of this little expedition," Janaina said. "He knows the area."

"With all of us beating the bush," Walker said, "he'll find us."

Grant thought it was odd how Marcos had become a ghost these last two days. Despite all the strange events, he'd been unseen by almost anyone in the camp. In Grant's experience, that kind of behavior always meant the person was up to his neck in something awful. And with the possibility of giant spiders on the loose, the last thing they needed was to stumble onto something else awful.

CHAPTER SIXTEEN

Grant put Marcos' Aztec book, a notebook and pencils into a backpack. Janaina handed him some packets of food and two bottles of water.

"Are we turning this into a picnic?" Grant said.

"I am afraid whatever is out there might turn this into a siege."

Grant grabbed two more ration packs and shoved them in the bag.

The two of them headed over to the crowd of men at the clearing's edge. Walker went from one to the next, doing some kind of inspection. The seventeen men carried a variety of axes and machete blades. Three had chainsaws slung across their backs. One of the bigger men in a red shirt shouldered the flamethrower Grant had seen used on the scrap wood pile.

"Bruno," Walker said to the man with the flamethrower, "you ready to haul that through the jungle?"

Bruno smiled with an unlit cigarette at the corner of his mouth. "Ready to roast me something large, no?"

Emiliano paced back and forth at the edge of the jungle, chopping the air with a machete. Blood stippled the bandage on his left shoulder. He didn't take his eyes off the broken trail that led away from where Janaina had found him.

Walker greeted Grant and Janaina, and then handed each a machete in a sheath. "You might need these."

"It's like Christmas morning in the Amazon," Grant said. The big blade felt even heavier than it looked. He hung it from his belt loop.

Janaina approached Emiliano. "Are you feeling okay?"

He stopped and stared into the jungle. "Well enough to get my brother back."

She touched his good shoulder. "I'm sure we will."

The muscles in Emiliano's neck relaxed a bit. He looked her in the eyes for the first time. "I...I hope you're right. It's my fault he's out there. I made him leave. Scared him with a story of a demon, then got him attacked by something even worse."

"All right!" Walker shouted. "We're going in to kill whatever marched through camp last night. You had friends that died. It's payback time. Emiliano says it's a giant spider."

Men in the group gasped with fear.

"If it is, that's great." Walker brandished a machete. "Spiders chop up real nice."

Bruno waved the flamethrower wand in the air and whooped. "And I will light the grill to cook the pieces!"

Two men laughed. The rest didn't. Grant wondered if they all spoke English.

Walker turned to Emiliano. "Take us in, son. Back track the trail you took. Get us to that orchid wall."

Emiliano nodded and entered the jungle. The rest of the group gave each other tentative glances. Bruno snorted at them and followed Emiliano. One by one, the rest followed. Walker joined the procession with Grant and Janaina behind him.

"These men aren't warriors," Grant said to Walker.

"No," Walker said. "But when a fox is in the hen house, lots of chickens start to act like roosters."

***

An hour later, Emiliano wailed from the front of the column.

The group froze in place. Walker charged up to the head of the group. Grant and Janaina followed.

Emiliano was down on one knee, face buried in his hands, sobbing. The body of his brother Gabriel lay at his feet.

"Oh, hell," Walker said.

Gabriel was a bloody mess. Something had gnawed his extremities. There was a hole in his gut that exposed a jumble of internal organs. Flies buzzed in a cloud over the corpse. Blood coated the metal star that still hung from the chain around his neck.

Janaina went to Emiliano's side. She touched his neck from behind. "I'm so sorry," she whispered. She pulled him up. "Come away with me for a moment."

Emiliano did as she asked, apparently consumed in shock.

"Damn spider got him," Walker said.

"There's no webbing," Grant said. "And the body isn't drained and desiccated."

"The fella was being chased by a spider, and now he's dead. Don't need keen powers of deduction to solve that crime. All the more proof we need to kill that thing before it kills us."

Walker stepped away and started to tell the men about Gabriel. Grant gave the body a closer look. He waved away some flies with his hand. Scavengers had wasted no time getting to work, for certain. But the slashing wounds on Gabriel's body didn't look like an animal attack. They had the crisp signature of a man-made blade.

Over his shoulder, Janaina had brought Emiliano out of his shock and back into the real world.

"Let's move it out," Walker said.

Emiliano cast a sad glance at his dead brother. "I can't just…"

"We will bury him on the way back," Janaina said. "I promise."

Emiliano bent down and unhooked the chain with the star from around his brother's neck. He held it tight and started back down the trail. Walker and the rest of the group followed. Grant and Janaina took up the rear.

"That body didn't look like the other victims," Grant said.

"You don't think a spider killed him? The jungle is filled with other predators."

"Including a bipedal mammal variety."

***

A few kilometers later, Janaina nudged his shoulder. "Do you smell that?"

All Grant could smell was himself, and he wasn't about to win any aromatic prizes. He raised his head and sniffed the air.

Something special wafted through. Sweet, beautiful, powerful.

"Orchids?" he said.

"And many of them."

The group halted. Grant and Janaina worked their way forward to where Walker stood. A few meters ahead, the trail broke into a clearing. A line of trees with interlocked branches walled off the far end. Orchids studded the trees like Christmas ornaments. The air practically dripped with the flowers' cloying scent. A trail through the grasses led to a section of the orchid wall that had collapsed.

"I didn't know that orchids grew in groves like this," Grant said.

"They do not. This is not natural, to be lined up like this."

"Someone built, or planted, a wall to keep something out."

"Out of where?"

Emiliano stepped up. "This is the place." He pointed to a gray stone sticking up from the grasses at a low angle. "The Aztec warning."

"All right," Walker said. "Spread out around the stone and that opening in the wall. Keep an eye on the jungle."

Grant and Janaina approached the stela. He pulled away the grass for a better look. A long string of complex symbols covered the sides.

"You can translate that, no?" Janaina said.

"Sure, right off the top of my head," he said. "I didn't even need to bring the Aztec translation book."

"I think you are not serious now."

"Now *you* think correctly."

There was no way he was going to be able to transcribe the inscription on the spot. He took the pad of paper and the pencil out from his pack. Sheet after sheet, he laid pages on the stela and traced the outlines of the symbols carved beneath.

"There are a lot of snake symbols there," Janaina said.

Grant pointed to one glyph that unmistakably had eight legs. "And way too many of these as well."

A grating high-growl broke the silence. Then something crashed in the jungle behind them. Grant whirled around.

Branches flattened to the ground, then a spider two meters tall and twice as long stepped into the clearing. Thick black fur coated its body. Its head jerked sideways. Twin eyes black as polished obsidian seemed to lock on Grant.

"Oh, hell," Grant said.

Then a second spider appeared beside it.

"Great," Grant said. "Now it's a party."

CHAPTER SEVENTEEN

The men closest to the spiders yelled in surprise and retreated across the grassy perimeter.

One spider pursued. With each step, its eight legs seemed to hit the uneven ground in the perfect spot, and its body appeared to float as the spider closed on the slower men.

One worker tripped and went down. The spider pounced. Two glossy black mandibles the size of elephant tusks clamped on the screaming man. He shuddered and then went limp.

The other spider barreled into the clearing toward Grant and Janaina. Janaina sprinted for the opening in the orchid wall.

Grant hit the dirt and rolled under the stela's shadow. The spider passed him.

"Giant spiders," he said to himself. "Why does this crap keep happening to me?"

A few workers gathered to make a stand. The spider zeroed its gaze on the closest one. Then it spit a wad of webbing at the man. The beach ball sized web struck him at the knees and took him down. A filament from it stretched back to a spinneret somewhere under the spider's head. The web retracted and dragged the flailing man toward the spider's jaws.

Grant gripped the machete at his waist. "I'm going to regret this."

He rolled free of the stela, jumped to his feet, and drew the blade. The spider was just meters past him. He raised the machete and charged the spider from behind.

Two chainsaws roared to life to his left. With a whooping battle-cry, two workers sprinted to their comrade's defense. The spider launched a web ball at one and hit him square in the chest. The impact knocked him backwards. The chainsaw flew from his hands. He and the saw hit the ground. The saw sputtered to a stop. The man didn't move.

But that gave the second attacker the time he needed. He jammed the screaming saw against one of the spider's legs. Hair and green liquid sprayed from the spinning chain. The spider squealed. Then the saw choked to a halt.

Grant reached the spider. He brought his blade down on its leg in a great, sweeping arc.

The blade struck the leg like hitting a concrete wall. Grant's arms vibrated all the way to his shoulder. He released the machete. The spider's leg kicked out and sent him flying.

The spider spun to face the chainsaw-wielding worker. But Emiliano had scooped the fallen chainsaw from the ground and he joined the fray from the right. He throttled his saw to full and swiped at the spider's legs. The saw sliced through two in one pass. Viscous green fluid poured from the severed limbs like it came out of a spigot.

The spider swayed as it tried to maintain balance. The other man yanked the pull cord and restarted his jammed saw. The whirling chain severed the rest of the leg. The spider dropped to the ground with a deflating hiss.

Emiliano brought his saw down on the strand of web that held the victim to the spider. It severed the web. He stopped the saw, dropped it, and pulled the victim away from the spider. The webbed man looked catatonic.

The victory emboldened other workers. Machetes flashed in the tropical sun and five men charged the first spider. It looked up from feeding on its victim, then bounced up on all eight legs.

In rapid succession it fired web balls at three of the men. All hit dead center. Two of the three men were driven to the ground. The third spun on impact, which sent his growling chainsaw into the torso of a fourth man. They both hit the ground screaming.

The other man stopped short, as if realizing their attack force was down to him. He looked at the machete in his hands, and beat a rapid retreat.

The spider launched a strand of webbing at the closest man on the ground. He shouted and tried to break free, but the web ball had stuck his arms to his sides and his legs twisted apart. The spider retracted the webbing and the man bounced across the ground until he stopped under the spider's mandibles. The two black curves clamped down and lanced the man's body. He shrieked and went silent.

From the far end of the clearing came a rifle shot, then another. Walker stood there, rifle to his shoulder, aiming at the world's biggest arachnid. He fired again. None of the bullets seemed to hit their mark.

Then a whoop like a screaming monkey ripped through the air. Bruno burst from the tall grass, pointing the flamethrower, and charged the spider. The heavy tanks slammed up and down against his back with every stride. Flames bubbled at the end of the wand and drips of liquid fire left a trail behind him. Meters from the beast he took a knee and braced the wand against his chest. He aimed at the arachnid.

He pulled the trigger and a flaming stream rocketed out of the wand. It hit the side of the spider. The creature screeched and jerked the dead worker back and forth in its mandibles.

The fiery assault appeared to be more than the spider wanted to endure. It scrambled back into the jungle with the dead worker in its mouth. Smoke trailed from the singed hair along its side.

Grant touched his chest where the spider had struck him. Nothing seemed broken but the bruised area had already started to swell. "What do you know. Still not dead."

He grabbed the edge of the stela and pulled himself to his feet. Janaina came running from the wall.

"Are you okay?" she asked. "I thought you were right behind me."

Janaina stepped closer to the dead spider. The stench coming off it practically clouded the air. "The man with the chainsaw finally stopped it."

Grant stepped over and pulled his machete from the ground beside the spider's leg. "Well, sure, after I mortally wounded it, it was easy pickings."

Walker rounded up the surviving workers and sent them to the opening in the wall. Grant and Janaina checked the corpse the first spider had left behind. The body had the same desiccated features and gray flesh as the victim of the barge incident.

"I think it proves we weren't visited by a jaguar last night," Grant said.

"Never thought I would be unhappy that a jaguar didn't attack," Janaina said.

CHAPTER EIGHTEEN

Walker came up behind them. The rifle hung on his shoulder. Sweat rolled down the sides of his ashen face.

"Are you okay?" he asked Grant.

"Way better than that guy," Grant said, pointing at the shriveled corpse on the ground. "Who likely died of a jaguar attack according to your previous diagnosis. I need to brush you up on the difference between felines and arachnids when I have time."

"Okay, I didn't reckon giant spiders made a lot of sense. Looks like I was wrong there. Where the hell would giant spiders come from, anyway?"

"Millions of years ago, the same environment that supported that fossilized giant snake could certainly support giant spiders."

"This discovery must make you damn happy."

"No, believe it or not, I like my giant monsters at least a million years more dead than those things."

"How can they be here in the jungle?" Janaina said. "This place, it is not isolated. People would have encountered them, especially aboriginal people. The tribes have no stories, or even myths, about giant spiders."

She was right. Their secret existence did not make sense. Especially for something so big. "They must have been isolated by something else. Finally able to cross a falling river, allowed access out of a gorge."

"The water levels are the same," Walker said. "And there ain't no gorges around."

"Something had to keep them away from the rest of the world," Grant said. Then it hit him. "The wall behind us. We assumed it was built to keep something out."

"But instead it kept something in," Janaina said.

"And I have etchings of the glyphs on the stela. Translating those might tell us if we're right."

"Well, I'd say we use the wall to our advantage. We pull everyone back behind it, put as much of it back up as possible."

"And hope that all the spiders left when the wall opened up," Janaina said.

"The grass around the opening is pretty trampled," Grant said. "And the drive to explore new territory would be strong after being confined. There's a good chance the whole nest left."

Walker's mouth drooped. "You think there's more than two?"

"You ever seen how many babies spiders have?"

"Hell, well if we can at least narrow the gap in the wall, it looks like the flamethrower can hold them off."

Grant stepped over and crushed out a spot of burning grass. "If we don't incinerate ourselves in the bargain."

***

The group retreated behind the wall. The broken section needed to be repaired, and this was just the crew to do it. They felled trees from within the perimeter and through a show of teamwork and brute strength, raised the orchid–laden collapsed section and braced it in place. That still left an opening big enough for a spider to get through. They began to cut and stack trees to fill the gap in the wall.

Janaina took a quick look around the area inside the wall. Just as on the outside, a swath twenty meters wide was clear of everything but grasses, then the jungle took over. That was odd. Even if the spiders patrolled the wall for some reason, that wouldn't keep the rainforest from reasserting itself across this empty space. The arc of the wall implied that it was a circle, though how big a circle she could not guess.

From the inside it was clearer that the wall had been engineered by man. There were the remains of mahogany posts and collapsed holes from missing posts within the perimeter. The trees that had grown in place of the old wall had near identical spacing.

Emiliano sat alone under a wide tree, staring at the ground. Blood stained the bandage at his shoulder. Janaina went to him.

"I am so sorry about your brother," she said.

"I was supposed to look out for him. It was my fault he was out here in the first place."

"How could you know there were giant spiders in the jungle?"

He looked up at her, eyes filled with anger. "He was not killed by a spider. We both saw that. He escaped the spider, and someone killed him after that."

"Who would do that?"

"The only man missing from camp this morning."

Indeed, Marcos had been missing since they'd arisen. But the strange little man would have no reason to kill Gabriel if the two of them somehow stumbled into each other in the jungle.

"There are other explanations," Janaina reasoned. "Other predators in the Amazon. I have seen many."

Emiliano jabbed his machete into the ground and held it with an iron grip. "There is only one predator I will be looking for."

Janaina realized she wasn't going to convince him otherwise, and that she wasn't sure she should. She touched his hand on the machete. It relaxed.

She headed over to Grant. He sat a dozen meters from the entrance, back up against a tree. His tracings sat in his lap, the Aztec book open beside him.

Janaina sighed in frustration and turned to Grant. "What do the inscriptions say?"

"I'm going to caveat this with saying the only thing I ever translated into English was high school French, and the only phrase I mastered was asking for the restroom. Also, the glyphs are much more like strung together words and stories, as far as I can make out, so syntax is out the window."

"So you are saying you are bad at this."

"In a much nicer way, yes."

Grant laid out the pages he'd been using to transcribe the hieroglyphs. He pointed to them as he spoke.

"The stela is a warning from King Axayacatl to avoid the lands beyond. They were cursed by Tizcatl, the Viper King, whoever that was."

"Axayacatl was an Aztec King," Janaina said, eyebrows arched in excitement. "Tizcatl was a half-brother who tried for the throne and was exiled. Schoolchildren know these things."

"Maybe we should get some of them in here to translate this thing."

Janaina flicked his shoulder with her finger. "Sarcasm Man, this is a huge archeological find."

"Sorry, fossils are what light my fire. All of this seems so…recent…compared to what I usually uncover." He pointed to an image of a snake. "It praises Axayacatl for defeating the demon creatures commanded by the Viper King, and trapping them in the city. The

THE CURSE OF THE VIPER KING

warning seems to say that any trespassers risk awakening the Viper King's demons behind the wall."

"Do you believe in mythical demons?" Janaina asked.

"I suddenly believe in giant spiders," Grant said, "So I'm kind of open to anything right now." He pointed to another glyph. "What's to say the Viper King didn't somehow use giant spiders against Axayacatl the way Hannibal used elephants against the Romans?"

"How can a wall keep climbing spiders inside?" Janaina said.

"These spiders may not climb. First they are too heavy. Second they look more like ground spiders. Modern trapdoor spiders are pretty much terrestrial."

"Even so, they might dig under a wall, or something else might. The smell of the orchids would attract other animals as it did us."

"Or just the opposite. The orchids could repel them. Who knows what a spider thinks smells good?"

"There's no arguing one thing. The wall came down and now there are giant spiders."

Just then Walker stepped out of the jungle. He had Marcos at his side. The botanist was dirty enough to have spent a week in the jungle.

"Well," Janaina said. "How you say, look what the bat dragged in."

"Cat," Grant said. "What the cat dragged in."

Walker brought Marcos over to them. "I found our missing botanist."

"I was scouting the area beyond that tree wall for mahogany stands," Marcos said, "heard the chainsaws and the screaming, and was very surprised to find all of you so far from camp."

"More surprised than seeing us fighting giant spiders?" Grant said. "And I was surprised to find that you'd left camp this morning after the spider attack last night."

"I slept through that, and left at dawn, not knowing anything had happened."

Janaina cast a sideways glance at Grant. He looked no more convinced of Marcos' story than she was.

"You!" Emiliano shouted from across the clearing. He jumped to his feet and sprinted for Marcos, machete swept up and back over his shoulder.

As Emiliano closed on the group, Walker crossed his chest with his rifle and blocked Emiliano's way. "Whoa there, son. What's wrong with you?"

Emiliano skidded to a stop. "He killed my brother!"

"I have no idea what he's talking about," Marcos said.

"A spider killed his brother," Walker explained to Marcos.

"It didn't look that way," Grant said.

"Not likely any of us are experts on giant spider killings," Walker said. "The boy may have died a dozen ways, but I don't think a botanist did it."

"Certainly not," Marcos said. "You are the first people I've seen all day."

Janaina didn't like Marcos' dishonest vibe. And it was clear that Emiliano wasn't buying the botanist's story either. His grip on his machete tightened until his knuckles turned white.

"Calm yourself down," Walker said to Emiliano. "Marcos didn't kill your brother any more than I did. You've been through a shock. Now head back to help guard the entrance."

Walker gave the rifle a light press against Emiliano's chest. Enough to send the message that his statement was an order, not a request.

Emiliano backed away, but the fury on his face didn't lessen. He took up a spot near the wall.

"Is it just me," Grant said to Marcos, "or do you just bring out the best in people?"

"What did you find further in the jungle?" Janaina said.

"More jungle," Marcos said. "And no stands of mahogany worth harvesting."

"There go my hopes you'd found a Starbucks," Grant said. "I thought they were everywhere."

"Can you be serious for a damn second?" Walker said.

"Sure," Grant said. "We're trapped inside a wall with no resources, surrounded by giant spiders, with machetes as our primary defense. That serious enough for you?"

"We're not getting back to camp before dusk," Walker said. "And I sure as hell ain't walking through a rainforest in the dark, especially with who knows how many giant spiders out there."

"Or in here," Janaina added.

"I've been within the wall all day," Marcos said. "Haven't seen anything like that."

"They're hard to miss," Grant said.

"Then we'll finish reinforcing the opening in the wall and bed down for the night here," Walker said. "I'll pass the word." He and Marcos headed off together.

"He thinks that we will be safer in here," Janaina said. "I am not sure of that."

"Maybe that was his sarcasm voice," Grant said. He looked over at the men who had returned to building the barricade. "I hope that wall is spider-proof."

CHAPTER NINETEEN

The coming night raised the group's anxiety level. Everyone had planned to be back in camp by dark. Few had brought any food. One of the men had found a clear stream so the threat of dehydration was kept at bay, but it would be a night under the stars, or the canopy if someone chose the jungle over the clearing around the perimeter wall.

Grant watched from the edge of the tree line as the shadows grew long. The men had felled a few more trees and finished blocking the only opening in the wall, at least the only opening any of them knew of. The pile wasn't as strong as the living wall elsewhere, but it provided way more comfort than a gaping hole.

With the job complete, the workers had camped out in a rough circle in the clearing, around a mid-sized fire. Without the familiar task of felling trees to occupy them, it seemed that their situation weighed more heavily upon them. They spoke among themselves in low tones, nervously handling their machetes and saws. Any noise from outside the wall sent heads swiveling in the direction of the new barricade blocking the opening to the outside world.

Grant pondered that these men were not of the same stock as the Aztec warriors who had left the stela and presumably built the wall. They were simple people cutting timber as a way to get by, now in completely over their heads, and well aware of it.

Bruno with the flamethrower was the only exception. He sat atop the barricade, keen eyes trained on the clearing beyond. He'd relished the fight and was ready for more. Grant hoped he'd inspire the rest.

Walker and Marcos had settled into a niche inside the tree line. Grant returned to where he and Janaina had staked out a mossy spot under a low palm. No one in the party had been anything but civil to Janaina, but Grant still felt more comfortable with both of them set off from the others. Something about that meant he feared human beings as much as giant spiders, but he didn't want to dwell on the idea. The low buzz of the men's conversation traveled across the clearing, human voices at odds with the buzz and chirp of the rainforest.

"They feel the safety in numbers against predators," Grant said.

"And take comfort in the fire against the darkness," Janaina said. "Ten thousand years of evolution and there are some things that we still react to just the same. The native peoples here, they are the same. The village is an indivisible unit. The fire something to be tended and kept burning."

"How advanced were the Aztecs that set this place up?"

"Likely as advanced as Ancient Rome. They built great roads, huge cities, understood irrigation."

"And lived more peaceably."

"Oh, not at all. Warfare among the sects was constant, political rivalries fierce. And victors got the spoils, losers got a beheading."

"Then I'm guessing that it didn't pay to be the Viper King."

"His half-brother would have been ruthless in his revenge. But this wall that we see, this is different, how you say, the cow in the hen house."

"Actually, we don't say anything like that at all, but I get the point. Why is this so different?"

"Rival cities would be conquered, and either occupied or razed to the ground," Janaina said. "The stela says that the Viper King and his demons were walled off inside."

"Like big brother couldn't conquer the city."

"Or would not risk trying."

"That means there's a city inside this wall. Marcos said there's nothing but jungle."

"I do not trust Marcos to be truthful."

"Walker believes him."

"Because he finds Walker the mahogany. There is something deeper in the jungle that he wants to keep hidden."

"And I suppose you think we should go find it?"

"Very much so."

Grant looked into the rainforest. The setting sun had spawned impenetrable darkness. No way he was braving that after the day he'd had. "We shouldn't leave now. I just ordered room service."

"We should go in the morning."

"Splendid idea. And yes, that is my sarcasm voice."

CHAPTER TWENTY

Marcos' watch buzzed him awake.

The jungle was still pitch dark. He checked the watch's display. 5:30 AM.

Perfect, he thought. Before dawn awakened any of the others, he'd be long gone.

He clicked on a blue-tinted penlight and stood up. Joints creaked a dozen different ways from sleeping on the hard ground. A jab of pain lanced his neck and he swatted away some unknown insect. He swore he'd never live like this again. He knew that after today, he'd never have to.

He picked his way through the plants and gave a wide berth to the sleeping forms of Grant and Janaina. He wasn't worried about the workers from the camp screwing up his plan. But these two…wild cards in the deck. No way the paleontologist would let the discovery of the city of the Viper King remain a secret. And even before they got back to the real world, the woman would be a major problem. The way she reacted to his interest in the Aztec past, and paraded her devotion to the Stone Age natives who scraped by in this godforsaken hell-hole, she had the potential to wreck his plan before he even got it rolling.

He gripped the machete in his belt. He could take care of that problem right now. He'd taken care of Gabriel. One quick blow to the neck apiece and they wouldn't be talking to anyone about anything.

But Gabriel hadn't died with one quick chop. At the first blow, the woman would scream. By the second, Grant would be up in her defense. By the third…

He let loose the machete handle. He'd have to let them live another day.

Thoughts of Gabriel brought back memories of his brother Emiliano's attempted assault. How had Emiliano known he'd killed the man's brother? Had he left a clue? How had anyone even found the body in this vast rainforest?

He shook off his concerns. There couldn't have been any proof. Walker would vouch for him against any later wild accusations. Provided anyone other than himself made it out of this jungle to try and press any charges.

He made his way to the clearing around the perimeter wall. The route to the lost temple would be longer this way, but faster and safer than picking his way through the rainforest at night. Even with the detour, by dawn he'd be back at work, and by dusk he would have his prize.

**

Grant's eyes snapped open. He sat straight up, wide awake.

The jungle was quiet. But he was certain that a noise had awoken him. A creepier thought came, that he'd been awakened by a presence.

He checked on Janaina. She still slept on the other side of the tree. Something glowed atop her body. He bent down for a closer look.

Two orchids had blown from the wall and landed atop her. In any other situation, it would have been adorable.

Grant checked his watch. It was almost dawn and the first promise of the sunrise had added a rosy glow to the eastern sky over the clearing. Sleep wasn't going to happen again, so he opted to get up. He rose and groaned as his body straightened up.

"Three college degrees," he whispered to himself, "and I'm sleeping in the dirt. What's wrong with this picture?"

With silent, delicate steps he made his way to the clearing. The fire the workers circled still glowed, though the flames were long gone. All but two slept around it. Orchids had dropped over and around their bodies as well.

Bruno sat up against the reinforced barricade, next to the twin steel fuel tanks. He smoked a cigarette and the red tip glowed as he inhaled. There had to be something drastically unsafe about smoking next to flamethrower fuel tanks. But surrounded by giant spiders, safety was really a relative thing.

Emiliano sat atop the pile, eyes focused on the clearing beyond the wall. He looked haunted. Grant could understand why.

Behind Grant, leaves crunched. He whipped around to see Janaina standing behind him.

"Damn! Don't sneak up on me like that."

"I will crash about more next time." She handed him the two orchids that had landed on her overnight. "Our relationship, it is not ready for you to bring me flowers."

"I get no credit there. Blame the breeze." He pointed to the sleeping men around the fire. "It blew them everywhere."

Janaina looked past them to Emiliano at the wall. "Do you think Emiliano slept?"

"After finding his dead brother, I doubt it."

Walker stepped up beside them and yawned. "Good morning, y'all."

"Another day in a tropical Eden," Grant said. He looked behind Walker. "Where's Marcos?"

"You haven't seen him? He was up before I woke up. Yesterday he mentioned checking the perimeter of the enclosure. Maybe he got a jump on it."

"You do not keep track of him well," Janaina said. "It does not worry you that he is missing?"

"I'm sure that if something came in and carried him off, at least one of us would have woken up. He's been in and out since the first day we arrived, always out scouting the area. He's always brought back the locations of the best stands, identified places to avoid. Didn't really need to be bird dogged."

"I am no management expert," Janaina said, "but I think you need to watch him."

"You're right," Walker said. His eyes narrowed. "You're no management expert. In fact, you two aren't even supposed to be here at all. I'll take care of my crew as I think best. You good with that?"

Grant took Janaina's shoulders and walked them both back one step. "You got it, boss. No problem."

Walker headed over to the men around the fire and started to set them to different tasks.

"You are like a magician," Grant said to Janaina. "Poof! Friend into enemy."

"But you agreed that Marcos is hiding secrets, and now he is missing before daylight breaks."

"But Walker trusts him so there's no point in strangers trying to break that bond. We'll need to keep an eye on him ourselves."

"You mean we go look for him?"

"And the city the stela tells about. If you are up for it."

"I thought you'd never ask."

CHAPTER TWENTY-ONE

Emiliano slapped at an insect on his forearm. He pulled his hand away and revealed a splotch of bright red blood.

One blood-sucker down, and Marcos to go, he thought.

He rubbed his brother's star between his fingers. The bulky chain hung heavy from the pendant and rubbed against his knee. He didn't care what the others believed. He knew what had happened to his brother, and he knew who did it. He'd get revenge.

Of course, he'd have to stay alive long enough to exact his revenge. The rising sun sent the humidity into overdrive and sweat seemed to seep from every pore in his body. From the top of the barricade, he looked out across the clearing. The dead spider lay in the open like the remains of a wrecked warship. Deadly in its time, but now just a horrific reminder. How many more were waiting in the jungle for the men to venture out beyond the wall's protection?

Janaina climbed up beside him. He broke into a smile. He'd met good and bad throughout his life, and had come to recognize good in the rare instances he found it. This woman had a big heart and a kindness rarely seen, especially at a jungle logging camp.

"Holding up okay?" she said.

He clamped both hands around Gabriel's star. "So far so good."

"I'm so sorry about your brother."

"Not as sorry as Marcos will be."

"We're going to get out of here. But we're going to have to do it together. Fight the spiders instead of each other."

"I know what he did."

"And we will make him pay for it later." Janaina pointed out across the clearing to where spiders no doubt waited in the trees. "But first things must be first."

Emiliano relaxed his grip on Gabriel's star. Janaina had a point. He had to focus on stopping one killer at a time.

"You are right." He wrapped the chain around Gabriel's star and placed it in Janaina's hand. "I gave this to Gabriel. It means the world to me. Keep it safe until we are all safe."

"No. You should keep it with you. It is your brother's."

"Holding it fills me with rage right now. Knowing it is safe will let me concentrate on keeping all of us safe, instead of on revenge."

Janaina held the star and chain to her chest. "I will guard it for you."

"Thank you."

Janaina slipped the star and chain into her pocket and climbed down the barricade. She passed Bruno climbing up. The big man had been wielding the flamethrower since they'd all left the camp. As a rule, he rarely showered and a night sleeping in the dirt had sent his personal stench into overdrive. Emiliano had never cared much for the man. He was the kind of bully that used to pick on poor Gabriel back when they were kids.

"See any bugs this morning?" Bruno said. His tone was one more of anticipation than fear.

"Not a thing."

"If they are dumb enough to come back, I'll be ready to light them up." He pulled a pack of cigarettes from his pocket and lit one. He blew out a cloud of smoke and smiled. "Smoked spider sandwiches for everyone."

The brute wasn't itching to fight to save others. He was itching to fight to kill.

Bullies are always bullies, Emiliano thought.

"Keep an eye out," Emiliano said. "Got to stretch my legs."

"And take a piss, right?" Bruno grinned.

Emiliano nodded. He really didn't need to do either, but he did need to put some space between himself and Bruno, for personal and olfactory reasons. He climbed down the makeshift barricade.

He saw Janaina and Grant just inside the tree line. Grant seemed okay as well, in a scientist kind of way. Emiliano didn't speak a lot of English, but the man seemed to say a lot of things that didn't make much sense. The two turned and disappeared into the jungle. That did not seem like a good idea. This was a time where there was definitely safety in numbers.

Suddenly, one of the workers came screaming out of the jungle, pulling up his pants. Emiliano recognized Rafael, the little Venezuelan who seemed able to climb trees like a monkey. Walker ran and intercepted him. Emiliano trotted over to the two. The terrified man pointed back into the jungle.

"Ghosts!" he said. "A cavern full of ghosts!"

"Don't talk nonsense, son," Walker said.

"I know what I saw," Rafael said. "I went to…relieve myself… and there was a cave. I stepped inside and… spirits floating in the air. Everywhere."

Bruno joined the trio. He'd shouldered the flamethrower tanks and looked ready to light something on fire. Walker grabbed the terrified man by the collar and dragged him back in the direction he'd just come.

"Show us these ghosts," Walker said.

Emiliano followed the three men down a path into the jungle. A dozen meters in, Rafael stopped short and yelped. The others bunched up behind him. Rafael pointed a trembling finger at a large hole in the ground. As Walker looked past the man, Rafael tore himself from Walker's grip and bolted for the clearing. He practically ran Emiliano down in his headlong rush to perceived safety.

Piles of fresh earth surrounded the hole.

"That's no cave," Walker said. "Something dug this out."

Something the size of those spiders, Emiliano thought.

Walker led the two men into the hole. It was shallow enough that the far end was visible. Threads of spider webbing crisscrossed the area. A mass of plate-sized white nodules clung to the center. Shadows moved within them, shadows shaped like spiders.

"Oh hell," Emiliano said. "These are spider eggs."

"Make that fried eggs," Bruno said.

He flicked a switch and flames appeared at the end of the wand. Before anyone could react, he sent a stream of fire into the center of the nest. It exploded into flame. A hundred screaming hisses sounded from the fireball. A stench like burned, rancid meat rolled up from the hole.

Emiliano's eyes watered as the heat made his face flush. Walker covered his nose and turned away.

A chorus of furious growls erupted from the other side of the wall. Emiliano looked back to the barricade and it was unmanned. Bruno had just wandered off without getting a replacement.

"C'mon," Walker yelled. He ran for the barricade with Bruno right behind.

One of the workers scrambled to the top of the barricade. His eyes grew huge as his face drained of color. He turned back to the others at the bottom of the barricade.

"Spider!" he screamed.

Emiliano ran to a closer section of the living wall. He popped a slit in it with his machete and peered through. He gasped.

There wasn't just one. An army of spiders ringed the clearing around the wall.

CHAPTER TWENTY-TWO

The spiders charged from the tree line. More of them than Emiliano wanted to count, all of them at least as large as the two they had tangled with outside the wall.

The spiders raced to the wall. But not all along it. They concentrated on the barricade the men had made around the opening, as if they knew that would be the weak point. And why wouldn't they? The rest of the wall had held them captive forever. It was as if an invisible funnel directed them all to where only the men of the logging camp barred their way.

A chain saw sputtered to life and the rest of the men scrambled up the barricade like an ant swarm. Walker shouted directions and fanned them out along the piles of felled timber. Emiliano left the wall and climbed the barricade to join the defense.

The first hairy spider leg wrapped over the barricade's edge. A worker on either side chopped at it with axes. The two blows severed the limb and a thick, green liquid gushed from the stump. The spider waved the wounded leg in the air and splattered blood across the men.

A second leg came over the top. It swept one of the axmen from the barricade. He tumbled backwards and landed with a gut-churning crunch on one of the lower logs. His back bent around the trunk at an angle no one could survive.

The spider's head rose like a dark moon, growling in fury, mandibles snapping back and forth, searching for prey.

The remaining axman charged through the spray from the wounded leg and with a mighty swing crashed the axe between the spider's eyes. It smashed through and the ax head buried itself inside the creature. The worker released it and the handle stuck from the spider like a canted unicorn horn.

The spider shuddered, then fell straight back. It bashed into a second spider and took that one with it down the barricade face.

The victorious axman turned to face the other defenders and raised a fist in victory.

A ball of webbing rocketed up from the barricade's far side. It struck him in the back and knocked him forward. He shouted in surprise and terror as he danced on the log to hold his balance. Then the strand of webbing attached to the ball snapped tight and retracted. It yanked the axman off his feet and straight down to the ground below.

Emiliano looked over the edge in time to see a spider swallow the man's head whole. He prayed to God that fall had killed the man first.

The first spider's failure did not deter the rest. Lined up like soldiers, they climbed the barricade in a mass of black, glistening fur. The men took positions along the top with machetes at the ready. Rafael had recharged his courage, and scrambled up the barricade with a chainsaw in hand. He stood dead center and fired it up. Walker was a third of the way to the top.

Two spiders crested the barricade together. Men hacked frantically at their legs with machetes. Unlike the axes, the lighter blades did superficial damage. Spiders at the base sent webbing balls flying and men fell screaming down both sides of the barricade.

From half-way up the wall Walker fired several rifle shots at the approaching spiders. They hit with splats of green blood, but did not slow the creatures.

Emiliano raised a machete to join the battle. Web balls struck him in the chest and hand. They knocked him back across the barricade's top. He tried to get up, but the webbing had glued his hand holding the machete to the trunk of a tree. He pulled but it was like being bound with steel.

Powered by bravery or insanity Rafael charged one spider head on between its front legs. He ripped the spinning chain across the creature's eyes. Ocher liquid the consistency of egg yolk poured from the wounds and the whirling chain turned it into a fine orange mist. Then he chopped through a leg and the spider rolled down the barricade.

But there were two to take the place of that one, and two more in reserve for each of those. Emiliano could see down both sides of the barricade. The men on his side of the wall would never stem the tide of giant spiders on the other. And the creatures would crawl over him to kill the other men.

One spider crawled straight up over two others. It mounted the barricade and raised half its body over the top. Its growl came out as a half-scream.

Then a stream of red fire blasted up the barricade like a comet's tail. It struck the spider on its less hairy, exposed underbelly. Its front four legs rose from the barricade as the spider reeled backwards. The rail of fire stopped, but the spider burned on, flames spreading from its chest to its sides. Black smoke spiraled from the flames' tips and the air filled with a smell like charred roadkill. The spider's head cocked to one side, and it rolled sideways down the barricade, flames spinning as it went.

"Broiled and served!" Bruno shouted. He stood halfway up the barricade. Liquid flame dripped from the flamethrower wand. He scaled the barricade without using his hands, jumping from one log to the next as he could not let the wand drop. The extra weight of the twin tanks on his back made him wobble a bit with each step up.

This fight needed everyone in it. Emiliano tugged harder at the webbing that pinned him to the tree trunk. The webbing didn't budge.

Bruno stood atop the barricade. He swept the nozzle of the wand back and forth and sent a torrent of fire down across the barricade's face. Flames hit the nearest spiders and their oily hairs lit up like a sea of candlewicks. One retreated and got as far as the edge of the jungle before collapsing in a pyre.

Another charged, as if knowing it was about to die meant it had to take its killer with it.

But the killer did not want to go. Bruno stood his ground without flinching. He bent at the knee to brace himself against the pressure and sent a streak of fire at the rushing spider.

The flames hit it straight in the face and immolated the entire head. The blood within must have boiled because a split-second later the entire head exploded, sending a rain of flaming parts in all directions. Bruno shouted obscenities at the spider and sent another stream of fire in the spider's direction.

Then a spider on the ground sent up a web ball. It hit Bruno in the head and encased him, like he'd donned some kind of faceless mask. He staggered forward and fell down the front of the barricade, with fire still streaming from the tip of the wand.

He landed with a crash against one of the tree trunks. The wand wedged into a crack between some logs. Bruno didn't move. Nor did his finger release the trigger.

Flames licked the random gaps between the barricade logs. The structure lit up like a pile of kindling in a fireplace.

The few surviving men tried to climb down the barricade. Fire belched through one opening as a man traversed it. He went up in a screaming, crimson flash. Another slipped and tumbled to a bone-breaking death.

The spiders on the other side growled and backed away from the growing flames. Emiliano cheered. Then he felt the heat of the flames beneath him start to sizzle away the sweat on his legs. He looked down and saw that the flamethrower fuel had dripped down to the base of the barricade, and the whole structure was about to become a bonfire.

With him stuck to the top.

CHAPTER TWENTY-THREE

Marcos scooped a shovelful of dirt from the earth. In the jungle humidity, sweat streamed from every pore and every labored breath felt thick. He launched the shovel's load up and out of the hole. The huge stone block over his head shifted. The thick post holding up the hanging end creaked as more weight shifted to it.

Finalmente, he rejoiced.

He maneuvered around the post, and climbed up the side of the hole using exposed roots as hand and footholds. Yesterday he'd managed to get over six feet down and almost as far under this base stone in the old Aztec pyramid. With the few feet he'd just added, it appeared that he'd dug enough.

He wiped his hands on his shorts and then mopped the sweat from his brow with his t-shirt sleeve. A mosquito buzzed his ear and he slapped it dead.

He'd been right about the old Aztec roadway. He'd been able to expose sections of it in the jungle and it had led him to his prize. Though now on the outside it did not look like much of a prize at all. Centuries had allowed the jungle to reclaim much of the old pyramid's surface. Fifty meters high and three hundred meters long on each side, in its heyday, the stair-step pyramid had been a wonder. It now appeared more like an overgrown hill. Trees sprouted from cracks between the stones. Strangler fig vines crisscrossed the exterior and green algae transformed the tan, stone surface into a riot of greenery. But it was what was inside that mattered.

Marcos had only cleared the surface around the one stone he'd been digging beneath. The hieroglyphs along the edge included the image of a giant snake and an inscription about the king buried within. This stone was the key, the final one put into place after the corpse of the Viper King had been interred within. This was the only way in.

Marcos had thought himself quite clever. Unable to move the stone, he opted to let it move itself. By supporting one end and excavating the soil out beneath it, when there was more stone suspended than resting on earth, all he needed to do was pull the supporting pole. The weight that thwarted him would now work in his favor. The stone would fall away and leave the passage to the interior open.

He grabbed the end of the rope, drew it tight, then dug in his heels and pulled. The post ground against the base of the stone, then fell away into the hole.

The block didn't move.

Marcos cursed under his breath. The idea of going back under and shoveling out more dirt from beneath the sagging stone seemed like courting death. Maybe if he put the post back in place first...

The end of the block dipped. A cascade of earth tumbled down beneath it. Stone ground against stone and, as if in slow motion, the block slid away and down into the hole. It hit the bottom with a thud. A dark, rectangular opening gaped from the pyramid.

Marcos slung his backpack over to the edge of the pit, stepped atop the tumbled block, and pulled a small flashlight from his pocket. He flicked it on. The passage extended deep into the pyramid, well beyond the flashlight's puny range.

Marcos' heart pounded with excitement. Everyone knew that pyramids were tombs, reserved for Aztec kings and princes. And the phrase "you can't take it with you" had no Aztec translation. They took it all with them. Gold, emeralds, silver. Cleaning this place out meant Marcos would never have to work again, never have to live in the sweaty dirt of the jungle, never be on the bottom rung of anyone's ladder.

He stepped into the passageway. The air was so stale it made him cough. It smelled of death: dead plants, dead animals, all desiccated over hundreds of years. Rows of Aztec glyphs covered the walls. He couldn't read them. He'd only learned the ones he'd needed to point him to the sealed entrance. What did he care about the life and times of some centuries-dead king? All that mattered was his accrued wealth, and its transfer into Marcos' backpack.

He worked his way down the corridor. To the right and left he passed circular passages three meters wide. Something had given the stone walls an irregular polish. They curved off, as if they circled the inside of the pyramid.

Behind him, the light of the entrance retreated to the size of a small box. The stink got a little better and he felt some motion in the air from up ahead.

The pyramid trembled. Just a bit of a vibration, but any motion in something this sturdy was disconcerting. Marcos froze and held his breath. Had the stone he'd removed made the pyramid unstable?

The structure stayed still.

Imagination, he thought. *Creepy places bring out creepy thoughts.*

All the same, he quickened his pace.

At the pyramid's center, the passage opened up to a square room. The ceiling seemed to extend all the way to the top of the pyramid. Dim light traveled down from four openings at the apex. The roots of strangler figs hung down from the top. Six round tunnel entrances gaped, evenly spaced, along the room's wall. In the center rose some kind of altar, with a statue that started behind it and rose three meters over the altar. At this distance he couldn't make out the carving at the statue's top. Behind the altar, a huge metal disc hung from the wall.

If I was the king, that's where I'd be buried.

Marcos headed to the altar. Something crunched under his feet. He stopped and played the flashlight along the ground. Dust billowed at his feet.

Human bones. Brittle from time, scattered around the altar's base. He'd read about Egyptian pharaohs being buried with their servants. Looked like this Aztec King had liked that idea.

He kicked through the bones. Most crumbled into fine dust.

The pyramid shuddered again. Stronger.

Marcos couldn't rationalize that one away. Maybe he had upset some delicate balance by removing that stone. The last thing he wanted to do was have a collapse trap him in here with the Viper King. He needed to scoop up his plunder and get the hell out.

He shined the light on the altar. A gold statue of a snake a quarter meter tall sat in the center. Even covered in centuries of dust it sparkled in the light. He went to the altar and picked it up.

Solid gold. Worth a fortune, even if all he did was melt it down. He stuffed it in the cargo pocket of his pants.

He played his flashlight over the altar. Gold leaf trimmed the upper level. Above rose a statue of a snake's head, mouth open, fangs bared. Both of its eyes glowed green.

Emeralds the size of Marcos' fists. If those were all he found, he could live like a king for years.

Something shifted against stone. This time the sound clearly came from one of the tunnels.

Marcos scrambled up the side of the altar. The cold stone had a layer of slime that made him shudder. He pulled himself to the top. The snake statue rose above him.

The scraping from the tunnel grew louder, closer.

Marcos' heartrate spiked. He gripped the snake and started to climb. One foot slipped against the slick stone. He clamped both arms around the statue to keep from falling.

His foot again found purchase on the statue's scales. He shimmied up to just below the head. The eyes of the snake seemed to sparkle, calling him closer. He reached out to pry one loose.

A chilling hiss sounded below him, like a burst steam pipe but with a bass bellow added. The hairs on his arms went to attention.

He turned to see the broad head of a giant snake protruding from one of the tunnels. Its scales were a mottled green, its eyes bright yellow and split by black slits. A red forked tongue whipped two meters out and flicked against the altar's base. It hissed again and exhaled the stench of decay.

Marcos screamed. He lost his grip and plunged to the floor.

The snake was waiting.

CHAPTER TWENTY-FOUR

Emiliano felt like a pig on a spit.

The fire the flamethrower had started now burned out of control. The pyre now generated enough heat that even the fresh cut logs caught fire. And all that heat rose through the gaps in the barricade and threatened to roast Emiliano alive.

On the far side, the growing conflagration was more than the spiders wanted to tangle with. They stood away from the flames, but still gave the living flower wall a wide berth and milled about near the base of the barricade. Every now and then one darted forward, only to feel the heat of the fire and scramble back to cooler ground.

Emiliano would have rejoiced at the fire keeping the spiders at bay, except that it was about to turn him into smoked meat. The spider webbing kept his one arm plastered to the log beside him.

He kicked his legs hard to one side and rolled toward his pinned arm. The effort damn near dislocated his shoulder. He screamed at the pain. He reached over with his free hand and tried to pull away the webbing.

He couldn't even get a grip. It was as if the stuff dried like plaster after it hit its target. He maybe could chip away at it with the machete, if he'd had one in his free hand.

The temperature rose as the crackle of flames grew louder. He'd stopped sweating, which meant that either he was dehydrated or that the heat was evaporating the sweat as fast as he produced it. Either option was bad.

Something popped in the fire far below him. Whatever had just burst into flames sent a plume of acrid smoke up through the barricade. It seemed to reach down his throat and sear his lungs. He coughed. What little he could see turned blurry as the stinging smoke made his eyes start to water. He clutched at the webbing that imprisoned him, praying that the heat had melted it.

Still rock-hard. He rolled back against the log and closed his eyes.

Some pain, he thought. *Then I'll see Gabriel again.*

"Emiliano!" Someone called his name.

He looked up into the haze. A face hung over him, blurry and indistinct in his watery vision.

"Gabi?" he choked out.

The face moved closer, came into focus. Walker, with his face covered in a rag like a bank robber.

"Don't move!" The shirt muffled his shout, but Emiliano got it.

Walker raised an axe over his shoulder and brought it down hard against the log. He missed Emiliano's hand by millimeters, but he gave the webbing a direct hit. It tore in two. Emiliano yanked his hand free. His machete dropped from his numb fingers and clattered away into the barricade fire.

Walker pulled him to his feet. There was no need to say more, nor time to say it. They both scrambled across the barricade to the living wall. The heat was less intense further from the flames. They worked their way down the barricade edge to the ground.

One of the surviving workers rushed over to Emiliano with a container of water. Emiliano downed it in an instant. He looked at his pants and shirt. All singed like he'd been in a broiler. He guessed that in a way, he had. His back and the back of his legs crinkled as he moved. They were going to hurt like hell very soon.

"Thank you, sir," Emiliano said to Walker.

Walker pulled the rag down from his mouth. The smoke had blackened the area around his eyes like a raccoon's mask. "Couldn't let you die up there."

Five men stood around them. Rafael still had the chainsaw. Three held machetes. One held a big stick. It looked like these were all who remained.

"The fire is holding back the spiders," Emiliano said.

A log shifted in the barricade and sent up a shower of glowing cinders.

"But fires don't last forever," Walker said. "And we don't have the manpower or the tools to add to the barricade."

"When the barricade burns down, those spiders are coming in."

Walker appraised the burning pyre, then looked back at the six men. "Okay, here's the plan. Marcos told me he'd discovered a pyramid in the jungle, and he's there now. I'm going to go after him. Maybe something there can help us, maybe we can signal a plane from there, who knows. I want all of you to gather up anything useful, food, tools. Fill all the water bottles. We're heading into the jungle."

The men stared through him, faces white with fear. Emiliano could tell they weren't going anywhere. No one moved.

"Well?" Walker said.

The men looked at each other, shaking their heads.

"The wall comes down, I'm going out," one man said.

Several others nodded in approval.

"You'll never get past those spiders," Walker said.

The devil they knew in the spiders outside the wall was apparently better than the devils they didn't know in the dark confines of the rainforest. Emiliano knew whatever these walls surrounded was likely their only hope.

"I don't think they're going anywhere, Boss," Emiliano said.

Little Rafael stepped forward, chainsaw in hand. "I'm with you, Boss."

Walker shook his head in frustration. "And you?"

"Trying to get past giant spiders is suicide," Emiliano said. "I say find the pyramid."

"Okay. Then stay here as long as you can. When the wall is in danger of breaching, follow the trail I use into the jungle. You can warn the rest of us they are coming, and hopefully we'll have found someplace safe by then." He pointed to the others. "Bring them when they smarten up."

"Roger that, Boss."

Walker slung his rifle. He and Rafael headed back to the tree line, and then disappeared into the jungle.

The other four men looked to Emiliano like he was the crazy one.

Emiliano wondered if he was.

CHAPTER TWENTY-FIVE

Grant led Janaina down a westward trail through the jungle.

"Are you certain we are going in the right direction?" Janaina said.

"Absolutely," Grant said.

"I am not believing you. Your face does not appear certain."

"My face is a liar. Trust my tentative positive response instead."

"I do not see any signs that Marcos passed this way."

"That's true. He made a mess hacking his way through the jungle to get here. The fact that there's no sign of that means he had to follow this trail."

"I will be impressed with your reasoning if we find Marcos at the end of this trail."

Grant would be impressed if they found anything at the end of the trail.

Up ahead, a section of the trail had been dug away, like a pot hole. When they reached it they paused. The excavated earth exposed a series of stones that matched the ancient roadway they'd seen before.

"There you go," Grant said. "Proof Marcos came this way. He dug that away to expose the Aztec roadway."

"Or a tapir was rooting around for grubs."

"Wow. I'm racking up zero credit for my Sherlockian deductions here. Thanks for the support. But you'll have to admit that this road goes somewhere."

"It did at one time. By now that somewhere may be back to being nowhere."

"Marcos would not have headed back to 'nowhere' first thing this morning."

Janaina shook her head. "Something is very wrong with all of this here."

"Sure. Giant spiders."

"No, not just that. The wall of orchids. The clearing around the wall."

"The stela was specific about the Aztec King building all that."

"And it is unchanged after hundreds of years?"

Grant tapped the road surface with his foot. "This still is. So are Aztec cities all over Central America. Romans knew to spread salt on land to keep enemies from growing crops there in the future. The Aztecs would be smart enough to do the same around the wall to keep the jungle at bay. It wasn't exactly a manicured garden out there."

Janaina appeared to mull the idea. "Perhaps you are correct."

"The only intervention by man out here in the last several hundred years was Marcos knocking down part of the wall and letting the spiders loose."

"You think Marcos did that?"

"The cuts in the trees were fresh. And it is too much of a coincidence that Marcos wanders off exploring the same day that giant spiders arrive and destroy our camp."

"He will have many questions to answer."

The two continued on. A half hour later, the old road ended at its destination.

A great stair-step pyramid loomed before them, easily fifty meters high and hundreds of meters wide. The jungle had tried its best to subsume this intrusive creation of man, and mosses and small plants sprouted from every level. Ropes of strangler figs traversed the structure, as if trying to compress the blocks back into the earth from which they had been carved. Stands of orchids sprouted in the trees along the pyramid's edge.

They walked up to the pyramid's base. Grant scraped away a layer of moss from the stones. Hieroglyphs of snakes and Aztec royalty saw daylight for the first time in forever.

"Behold the temple of the Viper King," Grant said.

Janaina looked at the plants covering the exterior. "I have studied many aerial surveys. With all that growing on the pyramid, it is probably invisible from the air."

"Then we are the first to see this place in a long time. Well, second, because I'll bet Marcos is around here somewhere."

They began to work their way around the base, climbing over fallen stones and around trees.

"There would be much more to this city," Janaina said. "A temple would not stand alone. The rest would spread out for miles."

Grant looked around. "This kind of seems to be it."

They turned the pyramid's corner. A great hole lay at the center of the next side. One of the stones from the pyramid's base lay toppled inside the pit.

"This is the part where you give me credit for getting us here, right behind Marcos."

Janaina's face turned red. "Marcos! He is just a bastard treasure hunter. That is why he had no botany books."

They made their way to the pit. A shovel and Marcos' pack sat at the edge. Janaina stared into the opening the missing stone had created. Grant climbed down into the pit and examined the carvings in the stone. The glyphs were the same as the ones from the stela. He pulled out his translation sheet to double check.

"This inscription is very similar," he said." It tells of the king defeating the Viper King in battle, and sealing the vanquished in the only structure the king did not destroy."

"That is why there is no city."

"It says the Viper King was sealed in here with his greatest demon. And I'm guessing that wasn't some literary device for his murderous personality." Grant looked down at the footprints in the earth. "And this is Marcos' work. The pit is full of little weasel footprints."

Janaina looked over the edge with confusion. "I do not see these weasel prints. Just boots."

"Never mind." Grant climbed out of the pit and checked the inscriptions on the pyramid face. "These glyphs were all made by the Viper King, extolling his glorious victories."

"How you say, putting the spin on it."

"At a minimum, embellished propaganda for the city population. There are lots of spider glyphs, glyphs of people being eaten by spiders. Those things must have been his equivalent of battle tanks."

Janaina checked some glyphs on her side of the pyramid opening. "These show ritual sacrifice, with a pyramid and a giant snake, likely representing the Viper King." She looked up to the pyramid top. "This was not a temple, or home, or tomb of the Viper King. It was the place where victims were sacrificed to him."

"And the victorious Aztecs sealed the Viper King inside to die. Poetic justice."

"Surrounded by his own spiders so he could not escape."

"There may be answers inside to explain how he controlled those spiders," Grant said.

"Marcos is already in there."

"Unfortunately," Grant said, "and that's the second reason we need to go in."

CHAPTER TWENTY-SIX

One look down the corridor gave Grant serious misgivings about exploring the temple. A few meters from the opening the corridor went pitch black.

"That does *not* look inviting. I've had my fill of wandering into dark places."

Grant opened Marcos' backpack and prayed to find a flashlight. No such luck. Some food packets, a quarter-full bottle of water, a Mexican passport. He wondered what Marcos was up to that he thought he'd need his passport. Was he planning on plundering something from the temple and then trying to get downriver and home with it right away?

"Anything useful?" Janaina said.

Grant pulled out a battered smart phone. "There's this. Now we can order a pizza."

"A phone will not help us."

"Unless…" Grant turned on the phone. The cracked screen came to life. One of the icons looked like a flashlight. He touched it and the flash for the camera came on. "Ta da. Illumination."

"In we go."

They entered the pyramid opening. The musty air hung thick with humidity. The smell reminded Grant of the inside of a zoo reptile house. The decorative carvings along the corridor indicated that this had been a normal entrance until the victorious king had sealed it shut with the toppled stone. Lichen and mold mottled the surface. Some of the carvings had broken away and left little piles of chips and sand along the walls. Light diminished as they progressed down the passage. Grant moved the flashlight beam to the walls. The carvings contained more pictures of snakes and people being sacrificed.

"The ads for this resort need a little work," Grant said.

"They are to inspire terror," Janaina said, "to let the enemy know exactly what awaits ahead."

"I'd think that by now all the surprise had drained away."

A circular tunnel intersected the rectangular one they were in. Grant sent the light down the other passage. The smooth walls curved away in the distance.

"Which way do you think he went?" Janaina said.

Grant shined the light on the floor. The only footprints in the fine layer of dirt went down the main passage. "Looks like he went straight for whatever prize might be in the center of this thing." He shook his head. "You know what's better about digging up ten million year old footprints than chasing fresh ones? You're certain that whatever is at the end isn't still around to kill you."

They continued down the corridor, passing a number of other circular intersections. A dim light appeared up ahead. The corridor opened to a large, square room. A reverse-stair-step ceiling mirrored the pyramid's outside design and Grant knew that they were in the temple's center. At the very top, openings in the stone let in enough light that Grant could turn off the cell phone light. Strangler figs had invaded the sacred space through those slots and thick tendrils hung down almost to the floor. Not only were the plants wanting to pull the structure back down into the earth, they wanted to tear it apart on its way down. Above an altar at the room's center rose a stone statue of a snake.

"Wow," Janaina whispered.

She walked forward to the statue. She stumbled as something clattered against her feet. Grant flipped back on the flashlight. Bones surrounded the statue.

"The Viper King did a lot of sacrificing," Grant said.

Janaina bent down and sifted through the bones with her fingers. She picked up a string of carved jade and set it aside, then a gold hoop, then bone carved into the shape of a snake.

"These were not the usual sacrifice, stripped down for humiliation and then sent in alone to face execution. These were all people of means, perhaps the leaders of the city."

"The inscription said he was sealed in here with his greatest demons. Maybe the whole leadership was left to die."

"The inscription said *greatest demon*."

"Then one of these guys was a much bigger jerk than the rest."

Grant shined the light up at the statue's head. Two emerald eyes shined back.

"Holy…those have to be the biggest emeralds in the world. They would be worth a fortune. Can't believe Marcos didn't pry those out."

Janaina reached down and plucked a shredded tan shirt from the floor. Blood stained the sleeve.

"Looks like maybe he tried," she said, "and fell off. The statue tore his shirt free on the way down."

"If so, then he's still in here. The only set of footprints in the corridor headed in."

They worked their way around to the back of the altar. In the shadows, a giant metal plate hung from the wall. It measured several meters across. Trails of rust dripped from the flaking mounts that held it to the wall.

"Looks like a gong," Grant said.

He pulled his machete from his belt and struck the plate with the butt of the handle. The result wasn't quite a musical note, but the deep, bass response sent a vibration through Grant's gut. It echoed all around the inner chamber.

The pyramid rumbled.

"What did you do?" Janaina said.

"Nothing! You can't wake up a pyramid."

The walls rumbled again. A scraping sound exhaled from one of the circular tunnel exits in the wall.

"My experiences over the last two weeks tell me now is the time to run," Grant said.

Then the head of a giant snake thrust out of the hole. Its body filled the tunnel. The triangular head came to a point around the mouth. It hissed as it opened its mouth to display a huge set of gleaming white fangs.

Grant and Janaina bolted for the corridor exit. Bones scattered and crumbled under their feet. A long forked tongue slithered out of the snake's mouth. It cocked its head in their direction and pursued.

Janaina made it to the corridor entrance. Grant jumped through right behind her.

The snake's head slammed into the passage entrance. Stone exploded. A cloud of dust billowed out and coated Grant's back. He turned to see the snake's head wedged halfway into the corridor. It shook itself free and withdrew.

Grant snapped on the cell phone light. Janaina hadn't waited. She was meters ahead of him, hands out trying to feel her way along a wall at a dead run. Grant caught up with her.

They closed on an intersection with one of the circular tunnels. The pyramid rumbled to the right. Janaina dashed past the opening. Grant was two steps behind. As he passed the tunnel, a hiss roared from the opening, followed by a blast of warm, fetid air. Grant dove just as the great snake snapped its jaws shut on nothing in the corridor intersection. The creature's head cocked and it took a bead on Grant.

The corridor was too narrow for the snake to turn and pursue. It issued a frustrated hiss and charged ahead. The scaly body blew by Grant like a freight train.

Janaina reached down and helped him up. "Are you okay?"

"Yeah, still not dead."

He got to his feet and they broke for the end of the corridor. They approached the next intersection and Grant held her back short of the circular tunnel.

"Wait." He drew his machete and shed his pack from his back. Back against the corridor wall, he put an ear close to the opening. He swore he could hear breathing.

He tossed his pack across the opening. The snake's head burst from the tunnel, jaws wide open. They snapped shut a split second too late to catch the pack.

Grant pivoted into the center of the passage. He raised the machete over his head in both hands, and tensed to give this serpent a death blow. He brought the blade down with all his strength.

It felt like he hit a steel tube. The blade dropped from his stinging hands.

A small gash in the snake's scales oozed red blood. The snake shuddered and then charged ahead. It hurtled by until its tail ended the show.

Janaina grabbed Grant's tingling hand and pulled him forward. He scooped his machete up with the other. She grabbed his pack on the way and they charged for the rectangle of light up ahead.

They burst out of the pyramid and skidded to a stop, facing the barrel of Walker's rifle. Little Rafael stood beside him.

"Don't shoot!" Janaina said.

Walker lowered the gun. "What the hell is going on in there?"

"Giant snake," Grant said between breaths. "I taught it a lesson, though."

The pyramid rumbled from deep within. The sound of crunching stone echoed far down the corridor. Grant flashed the light down the entrance. All it lit up was an onrushing cloud of dust.

"Jump!" he shouted.

He dove to one side, pulling Janaina with him. A cloud of dust blew out of the corridor entrance and Walker dove the other way. Rafael dropped the chainsaw and froze, as if after witnessing giant spiders and horrible deaths, whatever was coming was one terror too many.

The snake rocketed out of the pyramid entrance in an explosion of stone. Fragments rained among them and the snake's head thrust through the dust cloud.

The terrified worker had no chance. Even if he'd been capable of attempting it, escape was impossible. The snake opened wide and then snapped its jaws shut on the man without stopping. It roared forward and vanished into the jungle to the sound of Rafael's diminished screams. The waving palms went still in the snake's wake.

Marcos' actions had now set two species of giant predators loose.

CHAPTER TWENTY-SEVEN

Grant rolled over and spit a mouthful of dirt into the air. "I didn't think I'd be able to say it, but things just got worse."

"That poor man," Janaina said, looking at the path the snake crushed through the jungle.

"What the hell was that?" Walker said.

"Professional opinion? Giant snake."

"Where did it come from? And tell me 'the pyramid' and I may shoot you."

"It was in there for centuries. It looked like the Viper King kept it in there, had the pyramid built specifically to house it, with tunnels for it and a central feeding location for human sacrifice."

"And how's it still alive after hundreds of years?"

"Snakes can hibernate, slow their metabolism down so much it's hard to tell they aren't dead. Who knows how long they can keep that up? There are openings at the top of the pyramid in the sacrifice room. Add in the stray jungle creature that falls in as a snack, and apparently the thing could live this long."

"Why'd y'all let it out?"

"*We* did not let it out," Janaina said. She pointed to the excavated stone. "That was your man Marcos' work."

"And you'll notice the snake enlarged the doorway on its own after that," Grant said.

The pyramid entrance was a shambles. Great stones teetered above the enlarged opening, ready to tumble down and reseal the structure for good.

"Marcos said he'd found some sort of building in the jungle," Walker said.

"And were you going to share that with us?"

"I would have, but the two of you snuck out of camp at dawn. Now what did you mean about a sacrifice room?"

"In the pyramid center," Grant said. "There is an altar with a statue of a giant snake with emerald eyes."

Walker's face lit up.

"It looks like the Viper King would bring the human sacrifice there and leave it for the snake," Grant continued. "Then the Viper King's Aztec conqueror left *him* there, along with all his nobility."

Janaina seemed to shake away the horror of seeing Rafael meeting his end. She turned to Walker. "Why aren't you still at the wall?"

"Spiders attacked after dawn. We fought 'em back, but lost a lot of the men. The barricade at the entrance is burning. When it burns down, the rest of the spiders are coming on in. And there's a lot of 'em. Both of you and Marcos were gone, so while the remaining men guarded the barricade, Rafael and I came to find you. Marcos ain't here?"

"We found what was left of him," Grant said. "He was the snake's first victim."

"Serves him right for trying to steal from this place," Janaina said.

"We need to get up someplace higher," Walker said, "where that snake won't sneak up on us if it comes back." He pointed to the far corner of the pyramid. "Why don't you climb up that side where this thing still looks stable? I'll check the chainsaw, and bring it up when I join you."

Grant looked up the pyramid's side. The blocks were over a meter tall. It would be more of a climb than a quick walk up some stairs. Exerting the effort still sounded better than sitting defenseless on the ground. "Let's go."

He and Janaina made their way down the pyramid's side, then started a climb near the corner. The moss and algae made the ascent messy and slick. Every stone seemed to be cut just the right height to make scaling it awkward, even with random strangler fig roots as handholds. Grant's belly scraped over each corner as he pulled himself up. After all this time in the Amazon, he thought that he really should have been thinner.

Janaina had a much easier time with the climb. She mentioned during their escape from the Trans Union expedition site that mountain climbing had been an earlier passion of hers. It showed in how effortlessly she seemed to scale the stones. She stopped a few levels above Grant.

"Does this seem high enough?" she said, looking out across the jungle.

Grant's heart pounded in his chest and he felt his face growing flush. "It had better be," he said.

He pulled himself up to Janaina's level and collapsed beside her. "I swear on a stack of Bibles that I'm getting into better shape the day I get home."

"I thought you were eating a triple cheeseburger when you got home."

"Well, yes. But right after that, I'm hitting the gym. Well, after the cheeseburger and a three day hot shower. Then straight to the gym."

The usual hum and screech of the jungle rolled up the pyramid side. Somehow a big slice of nature out there thought everything was normal. Grant leaned back against the stone.

"This is grim," Janaina said. "We are trapped inside the wall with a giant snake."

"Maybe when the barricade burns down, the spiders will let it out."

"Or they will come back in and we will have spiders and a snake inside the wall."

"With only machetes for our defense," Grant said.

"We also have Walker's rifle and chainsaw."

"I forgot those. Totally even fight now." Grant glanced down the side of the pyramid to see if Walker was on the way up yet. It was empty.

"Do you think he came here looking for us?" Grant said.

"Perhaps he came looking for Marcos first, and us if we were with Marcos."

"Would you do that if you were in charge? Leave the men at the burning barricade and go find Marcos?"

"No, if I were in charge I'd tell everyone to stop cutting trees and go home."

"Probably why Cruz do Sul didn't offer you the job."

Walker climbed up the pyramid side. He'd left the chainsaw at the pyramid base. When he arrived, he was a bit winded. That gave Grant a little ego boost.

"Chainsaw's undamaged," Walker said.

"But not ready to chop up a snake that big," Grant said.

"Doubt it could even get through the scales," Walker said.

"Maybe it won't come back," Janaina said.

"I'm certain it will," Grant said. "The snake has been living in this pyramid for hundreds of years, maybe its whole life. Like any wild animal that has always been captive, the vastness of the world will be intimidating. It will come back here for security. It also associates this location with food."

"Do we want to be here for the homecoming?" Walker said.

"If there was a way to close the door after it went back inside," Janaina said. "But I don't think that is possible."

"That side of the pyramid is unstable," Walker said. "I could drop some trees on it and collapse it."

"So we just hope it comes back, and slips inside for the night?" Grant said.

"Unless you want to go out looking for it."

Walker stood and moved down one step. He surveyed the trees at the base of the pyramid entrance. "I could partially cut that tree there, then cut that one and the one behind it. It'll topple into the first two, and they'll crash slam into the entrance. That will be a few thousand pounds, easy. Enough to bring the rest of the opening down in a pile."

"Let's make ourselves a snake trap," Grant said.

Walker headed down the pyramid side. Janaina gave Grant an unconvinced look, and followed Walker down.

To the east, smoke rolled up into the sky from where the barricade still burned, like a fuse sizzling down to a powder keg of giant spiders. Grant hoped they had time to trap the snake before they'd need to survive two attackers at once.

CHAPTER TWENTY-EIGHT

The heat from the burning barricade radiated in all directions. The men nervously watching the fire had to retreat halfway to the tree line to keep from feeling like baked fish. They'd salvaged some provisions, shouldered their packs, and were ready to run.

Emiliano sat atop the orchid wall a few dozen meters from the conflagration. Spiders congregated in the clearing below. He lost count after ten. They were bunched up at a healthy distance from the great pyre, scurrying back and forth, waiting for it to burn down so they could exact revenge on the people inside.

Beneath him, a log deep within the barricade snapped. A section of the fiery pile shifted downward. Sparks spewed upwards on billows of white smoke. Time was not on the side of the men on this side of the wall.

One of the spiders moved faster than the others, shuttling back and forth along the length of the barricade, as if impatient to make its assault. Then it turned away from the barricade, and charged the orchid wall.

The spider jumped and landed several meters up. Its legs dug into the thick growth and it hung vertically, directly under Emiliano.

Emiliano's heart leapt. He jumped to his feet, and drew his machete. If that thing climbed to the top, he'd have to hack it to death one limb at a time.

One hairy leg stretched out to advance. It touched an orchid. The reaction was instant. The spider retracted that leg and shook it like it was being electrocuted. Smoke rose from its foot and the stink of charred fur wafted up the wall. The spider wavered, then dropped down off the wall. It hit the ground on its back and growled. It managed to roll over, and then retreated, dragging the injured leg beneath it.

93

The orchids are spider poison! Emiliano thought. The wall made sense now, how it had kept the spiders at bay even though they should have been able to climb over it, why the spiders were obsessed with waiting for the barricade to burn down to get back inside. This could be the edge they needed.

Emiliano climbed down the inside of the wall. At the base, he plucked a handful of orchids. He ran to the men who sat at the edge of the tree line. A pile of cut palm leaves lay between them.

"There's hope! The orchids, they are poison to the spiders."

Only one of the men looked up at him. "That is nonsense. A harmless flower. You go attack the spiders with a flower." He held up a palm branch. "We will conceal ourselves in the wall, the spiders will pass, and we will run to safety."

"Safety where?"

"Back to the camp. The company will come to pick up the barge, and we will be there. The spiders will be in here."

"The spiders will hunt you down before you even get close to the opening." Emiliano scattered the orchids at the men's feet. He crushed one and rubbed it against his machete's blade. Then he rubbed another up and down his arms. "This will knock them back."

"You go attack the spider. We've seen how that works out. Most of us are dead because of it."

Something shuddered inside the burning barricade, like the earlier collapse of the crumbling branches, but louder, more sustained. The fear on the men's faces grew.

Emiliano ran back to the orchid wall. He plunged his machete through it and chopped away a slit of leaves.

The spiders had formed a line facing the barricade. As he watched, one fired a web ball into a log at the base. It struck beside several others, and a cable of webbing from the ball to the spider drew tight. A squad of spiders were tethered to a trunk at the barricade's base. Together, they took a step back.

"Oh, no," Emiliano said.

The webs stretched tight. Flames licked at the webbing edges, and Emiliano hoped the webs would catch, but the gooey strands refused. In sync, the spiders marched back.

The tree trunk broke free. It skittered across the clearing, spraying a trail of glowing embers. A low moan echoed inside the flaming barricade as the remaining weakened trees sagged under their own weight.

The other men got to their feet. One of them made the sign of the cross.

Then the barricade collapsed. Like an orange waterfall, it sent a river of burning timber out toward the spiders. Logs bounced and somersaulted through the air like fireworks gone mad. The spiders scattered to both sides.

When the tumult settled, a patchwork of flaming timbers covered the clearing before the wall. Fires still burned at the edges of the now exposed entrance. But through the center ran a black mass of charcoal, flecked with dots of glowing red.

The spiders had cleared a path in.

CHAPTER TWENTY-NINE

Spiders charged for the opening in the wall.

The men were outnumbered at least three-to-one. They were doomed if they didn't scatter. Emiliano ran for the jungle, screaming for them to follow him.

The other men had been caught unprepared. Their plan to hide within the wall as the spiders passed was not going to happen. And they all knew it. In panic, they bolted in different directions.

Spiders surged through the opening and split to hunt down each fleeing man.

The lead spider singled out one dumpy worker who seemed to be running in slow motion. It was on him in seconds. Its mandibles clamped around his waist and he shrieked in an unholy high pitch. The spider bit into him and his scream wound down as the life drained from his body.

Another worker made it to the wall and began to climb. At three meters up, a web ball hit him square in the back. He wrapped his arms around the branches in the wall. But the spider retracted the web that stretched to the ball, and the man was no match for it. He came flying off the wall and hit the ground with a crunch and a puff of dirt. The spider pounced on him.

Emiliano neared the tree line. A web ball rocketed across his path and stuck to a tree. The web attached to it went taut waist-high. He remembered being webbed to the barricade log. If he hit it, he'd never get free. But he couldn't stop.

Like a baseball player heading for second base, he slid under the strand of webbing. With the machete in his right hand, he had to lean to his left. His injured shoulder took the impact and he felt the fire of his wound re-opening. The webbing passed over him.

But then he skidded to a stop.

He rolled up on his knees and looked back. The attacking spider growled and leapt at him, hundreds of kilos wrapped in stinking black fur, baring glistening white fangs.

The spider landed and knocked Emiliano to the ground. Emiliano slashed at its underbelly. The blade cut skin and left a searing, bubbling gash. The spider's leg touched Emiliano's arm where he'd rubbed it with orchids. Spider fur shriveled and steamed.

The spider bounced back up and skittered backwards. Green blood dripped from the smoking gash in its underbelly. It wobbled on its legs.

Emiliano looked across the grassy area. Spiders hunched over the others, jabbing mandibles into their corpses. None had survived.

He realized he wouldn't either if he didn't get moving. The one he slashed might recover, or one of the others might get tired of sharing and want a meal to itself. And if he died, no one would warn the others the spiders were on the way, or tell them that the orchids could help to protect them. Then Janaina and the others' deaths at the spider's jaws would be his fault.

He sheathed his machete and grabbed his bleeding shoulder. Blood seeped through the bandage. He prayed it would clot again.

Somewhere ahead in the rainforest lay the temple of the Viper King. He set out on the trail he hoped would end at the pyramid. One wrong turn and he'd be too late to save them.

CHAPTER THIRTY

The chainsaw's howl stopped. Walker stepped back from the tree and looked proud of himself.

From his vantage point high on the side of the pyramid, Grant could see Walker's plan. The three trees he'd partially cut through were lined up like dominoes to the right of the opening. When he cut the one furthest from the pyramid, it would crash into the other two, and all three would land across the unstable pyramid entrance. The avalanche of stone and timber would seal the snake back in its home.

"This is, how you say, a Hail Maria," Janaina said.

"Close enough," Grant said. "But we can do this. Walker seems to know how to drop a tree where he wants it to go. We'll seal this snake up tight."

"And still we will face the spiders."

"First things first. I prefer to look at life one killer creature at a time, it that's okay with you."

Off into the jungle, a curve of trees swayed like the tip of a giant invisible finger ran through the rainforest.

"That's our boy," Grant said.

"Snake!" Janaina shouted down to Walker.

Walker waved in acknowledgement. He gave the wedge cut into the furthest tree one more quick inspection, then he retreated to a small shelter of cut branches he'd built earlier. He ducked inside. Hidden from the snake as it passed, he'd then emerge and cut the last few inches of the tree trunk to seal the serpent inside.

Grant and Janaina ducked low behind a mass of fig vines that covered the pyramid face. The ripple of the great snake slithering through the forest grew closer.

"Door's open," Grant whispered. "Come on in."

Trees close to the pyramid shook. Branches snapped like firecrackers. Then the snake's triangular head emerged from the tree line. Its yellow slit eyes seemed to glow against its slick, green scales. Its tongue slithered out and tasted the air, searching for danger, or prey. It headed for the pyramid entrance.

"Good boy," Grant whispered.

As it approached the pit Marcos had excavated, the snake veered right, toward the half-cut trees and Walker's hiding spot. Grant's jaw dropped.

Janaina caught her breath and grabbed Grant's arm. Her nails pinched his skin.

The snake cruised by one of the booby trap trees. It veered left and headed for Walker's palm leaf shelter, just meters away.

Grant struggled for something to do, some way to distract the snake. But he was so far away, with nothing at his disposal.

The snake closed on Walker's hiding spot. Its tongue flicked out again, sensory radar in rapid search mode. At the last second, the creature turned right again, back toward the pyramid opening. Its side grazed Walker's pile of brush. The snake nosed into the pyramid opening, flicked its tongue again, then turned and curled in the sun around Marcos' excavation pit. The end of its tail lay between Walker's hideout and the half-cut trees. One flick of the tail and Walker would be crushed.

"Oh, for the love of God," Grant said. "This screws the plan to hell."

"Yes, how you say, throws in a monkey ranch."

"We need to draw that thing inside." A very bad idea bubbled up in Grant's brain. "The dinner bell."

"What?"

"The big metal plate inside. When I hit it, it summoned the snake. The Viper King must have trained it to know when the human sacrifice was ready. Like any captive animal, this thing is used to being fed, not to hunting. When it hears that noise, it's going to head in for dinner."

"And you will be dinner."

"Not if I can help it. The snake will take the direct route in. I'll head up one of the circular tunnels to get back out. I'll be out before its tail makes it to the middle. Then the trees drop and problem solved."

"You sound confident that will work."

"At least I sound that way."

"I will go with you."

"No, as soon as the snake goes inside, you need to head down the pyramid and make sure Walker knows what I'm doing. I don't want him getting chainsaw-happy with me in there."

"I do not like this plan."

"Imagine how I feel about it. Have a better one?"

Janaina paused, then shook her head.

Below them, the snake curled so its head faced the jungle. Unless the thing went to sleep, Grant wasn't going to get a better shot at getting himself killed. Crouching low, he crept across the pyramid face.

The snake shifted position. Its body slid back and blocked the pyramid entrance.

"You have got to be kidding," Grant said to himself.

He looked over at the entrance the snake had torn apart as it had burst through from the pyramid. Every stone looked ready to topple down. Great strands of strangler fig hung over the opening. They almost touched the ground. Almost.

"When I get back, I am never setting foot off campus again."

He crawled across the pyramid face until he crouched above the opening. He picked his way down, stone by stone. He dropped onto one that had shifted to a forty-five degree angle. His shoes slipped against the mossy surface. He teetered and fell. As he slid toward the opening he grabbed the stone's sharp edge. The rock bit into his fingers. He held tight against the pain and stifled a scream he was sure would alert the snake beneath him. His feet found purchase. He pulled himself up and gave his heart a moment to calm down to a normal rate.

He looked over at Janaina. She stared at him from across the pyramid, eyes awash in panic. He gave her a reassuring wave. Her face relaxed.

Grant's foot slipped again. He fell hard on his side. He grasped for anything. His fingertips hit the stone corner and one nail tore to the quick. He hung on. Then he crawled on his belly to a more horizontal stone. When he got there, he hazarded another wave to Janaina. This time she didn't look relieved.

He kept crawling over teetering stones until he was halfway down the opening. Lengths of strangler figs dangled down from the edge. He picked one that was about as thick as his arm and gave it a few yanks. It held fast. He peered over the edge.

It looked like he was about three stories up. The fig ended about three meters from the ground. A jumble of jagged, broken stone awaited him at the bottom. A giant viper lay meters away from where he'd land.

What could go wrong?

He could lose his grip. He could burn through his strength. The fig vine could break. A stone could fall and crush him. He could break a leg on the final drop. He could have a heart attack thinking of all these outcomes and die right here.

The snake inhaled and its scales scratched against the pyramid base.

Too much thinking, too little doing, he thought. *As long as that doing doesn't include dying.*

He grabbed the vine with both hands and took a deep breath. This was going to hurt.

CHAPTER THIRTY-ONE

Grant's arms burned instantly.

Supporting his body weight was a hell of a lot harder than he'd expected, even with his legs wrapped around the fig vine. Long forgotten memories of gym class rope climbs came back with a vengeance. At least he was going down, with gravity in his favor. Going up would be a nightmare. If the vine hadn't been so rough, he'd have tried for a controlled slide down.

His knees clamped together as the end of the vine passed between them. He let himself down a bit more until the end of the vine tapped his chest. He ventured his first look down.

He hung in empty space in the center of the pyramid opening. His feet dangled over two meters from the jumble of stones below. It seemed like a mile. Over his shoulder, the snake blocked the pyramid entrance.

His biceps quivered. He was about to be out of strength, and time. He angled for the least uninviting stone below, and let go.

For a millisecond that seemed to last forever, he didn't fall. A brief hope of being granted a miraculous ability to float crossed his mind.

Then gravity won out. He dropped. The ground came up faster than he'd expected. And the stone below him wasn't anywhere near as flat as he thought.

This is going to end badly.

He hit the stone hard. He tried to flex his knees, but the left one did not cooperate. His ankle hit the stone at an angle and excruciating pain raced up to his knee.

Grant collapsed and slid sideways down the stone. The rough surface sanded his palms raw. He screamed into a clamped jaw to keep from arousing the snake. He hit the ground and lay still.

His ankle was screwed up. He reached down with his fingertips to feel how badly. Swollen like a grapefruit. But not broken that he could feel. His hands though, had a serious case of biker road rash. He popped a few of the larger bits of rock out with his fingernails.

"Still not dead," he whispered. "Could have been worse."

He checked the wall of green snakeskin that blocked the entrance. It hadn't moved. Whatever noise he'd made inadvertently trying to commit suicide hadn't been enough to stir its interest. He hoped the dinner bell would.

He pulled himself up and stood on his good leg. He put some pressure on his bad ankle. It exploded in pain. He bit his lower lip and moaned.

Leaning against the side of the corridor, he picked his way around the fallen stones, and then limped toward the sacrifice room. The corridor grew dark quickly, but the expanded opening let in far more light than before.

He passed by the first intersection with one of the circular corridors, the Snake Superhighway. The entrance collapse had not blocked either side. That meant they were clear as an escape route. Well, at least that part of the plan was working, and he'd need it because with this ankle, outrunning the snake wasn't going to happen.

He hobbled down the corridor. He felt his way along the wall, wincing each time he put much weight on his left foot.

He entered the sacrifice room. High above, the slits at the peak of the pyramid let in the light of a day he was more than ready to return to. More vines from the strangler fig drooped down from the openings, the rainforest's reminder any structure man might create, it would eventually consume.

Now that he knew what they were, the collection of bones around the central altar stood out, reminders of the room's purpose, and a purpose he did not want to experience firsthand. Skulls that had last uttered a word centuries ago screamed at him to turn, run, and escape their fate.

The circular tunnels at the room's side were still clear and he mentally marked his escape route. As soon as he saw that snake come in, he was heading out.

He limped around the altar with its great stone serpent centerpiece and made his way to the huge metal plate to its rear. A closer inspection revealed that it hung from two metal chains in the wall. At a position halfway up its side stood a balcony. He imagined that in his heyday, the Viper King and his entourage would pound the plate from there, then watch with sick glee as his giant pet consumed a sacrificial victim. That would be an ideal location from which he could call the snake, except his escape route was down here on the floor.

He needed something big to ring this dinner bell. There was probably some big bat up on that balcony, but there was no time to hunt around for that. Last time he'd used the butt of his machete, but he needed this thing to ring loud enough for the snake to hear it outside.

He scanned the floor. Nothing but dust and bones. One of the skulls still wore some kind of headdress. He stepped over and inspected it. Half Spanish-era helmet and half crown, the glyph of the Viper King was engraved in the center. Some kind of jewels encrusted the edge.

"Well, if it isn't the Viper King himself."

Grant stuck his fingers in the eye sockets and thumb in the nose cavity like he was grabbing a bowling ball. He lifted it up and the jawbone fell away. The helmet-crown stuck fast, glued by the mummified skin underneath it. He did a curl and brought it up to his shoulder. It had some serious heft.

The king had to have had a neck like a bull to wear this thing.

But it would be perfect, and fitting, for what he needed to do.

He limped over to the great plate. He leaned back and then swung the skull against the plate.

This time the gong sounded as designed. The room vibrated with a bass bong like the world's largest doorbell. The strangler fig vines over the snake statue swayed.

Grant hopped around to the front of the altar where he could get a clear view of the snake's return. There was still light at the tunnel's end. The distant sound of scraping scales rumbled down the corridor.

Grant looked up at the head of the snake statue. "Well, I'd like to say I enjoyed the visit, but…"

There was something different about the statue. The huge emeralds in its eyes were missing, leaving two black holes. New white scratches surrounded the edges.

"Now where the hell…?"

The corridor rumbled and the light at the other end winked out. A hiss rolled out of the corridor's entrance.

The snake was on its way to dinner. He did not want to be the entrée.

Grant bolted for the tunnel on his left. He plunged into the abyss and prayed it opened up behind the snake's tail.

CHAPTER THIRTY-TWO

Janaina held her breath as the snake nosed into the pyramid. Even she had heard the gong from outside the pyramid. She wondered if Grant had thrown his whole body against it. The snake slithered its way into the pyramid. Smaller stones rolled down its sides as it scraped the pyramid edges on the way in. At last the tail moved from in front of Walker's hiding spot and vanished into the pyramid.

Step One had actually worked. She was more worried about Step Two: Grant making it out alive.

Walker peered out from between the palm fronds and checked the entrance. Then he emerged and swung the chainsaw up to his chest. He pulled the cord. It sputtered instead of starting.

The blood drained from Janaina's face. It was too early. Didn't he see Grant climb in there? She had to tell him the plan, and give Grant time to get out.

"No!" she shouted.

She jumped from stone to stone, dancing around the strangler fig roots and stair-stepping down the pyramid face. Walker pulled the cord again. The saw coughed. He bent over it and fiddled with the choke and fuel mixture. Janaina bounded off the pyramid base and ran for Walker.

She stopped beside him. "Don't do that! Grant is still inside!"

"If only you were, too." Walker whirled and crashed the body of the chainsaw against Janaina's head. She saw stars and dropped to the ground.

"W-what are you doing?" Her speech came out slurred.

"Finishing what I came here for. Marcos and I had this temple ready to be plucked, with a cartel buyer in Mexico all lined up. Then you two showed up and clustered things up."

"You and he…"

"You bet. Found the bastard farming secret poppy plants near my logging site in Washington. We shared a mutual desire to get rich. One thing led to another, he murdered himself an opening on my team, and then filled it. Now your boyfriend and the snake are gonna die under that pile of rocks, you're gonna be the victim of an accident here, and then I'm leaving with a pocket full of emeralds."

He gave the saw a furious yank. It sputtered and then roared to life. The chain kicked into overdrive with the scream of sliding steel. Walker turned from her and laid the blade into the trunk of the tree. A stream of woodchips sprayed into the air.

Janaina could barely think straight. Her head pounded. The edges of her vision flickered between black and very hazy. The blatt of the chainsaw made her head ache even worse.

A jagged wedge was missing from the other side of the tree. As soon as Walker cut far enough through this side, the tree would fall, strike the others below it, and seal Grant in with the snake.

She couldn't overpower Walker. She wasn't even sure she could stand without falling over.

She couldn't stop Walker, but maybe she could stop the saw.

She reached in her pocket and pulled out Gabriel's star on the heavy, metal chain. Even that whirling saw blade wasn't going to chop through that without a fight.

Walker faced away from her, focused on slicing the tree. The blade churned through timber, centimeters from completing the cut.

She rose to her knees and threw the star and chain at the saw.

It hit the saw where the blade met the body. It wrapped around the blade and wedged between it and the body. The chain bit into metal links and stopped.

The saw kicked up out of the tree trunk and knocked Walker off-balance. The chain snapped and the end lashed his face. Blood sprayed from a jagged tear that ran from his forehead, across his eye, and down his right cheek. He screamed, dropped the saw and grabbed his face. He sank to his knees.

Janaina got up and tried to run for the entrance, to warn Grant to get out. Instead she staggered. The pyramid canted left and then right, like she was on a ship in rough seas. She stumbled past Walker to the other side of the tree.

Walker's bloody hand shot out, grabbed her ankle, and yanked. Her head did another cartwheel and she hit the ground hard. Ice-picks of pain pierced her skull.

Walker crawled up over her. His face loomed over hers. Blood dripped off the tip of his nose and onto her cheek.

"You stupid bitch! Look what you done to me." Walker clamped a hand against her throat. "I'm gonna finish that tree with the axe. But first I'm gonna finish you."

Behind them, the tree made a loud, sharp, crack. Walker's head spun to check the sound.

Janaina took her shot. She launched her knee up into his crotch. He moaned and released her neck. She nailed him again. He rolled off her to the left and into the fetal position.

The tree made another, louder, longer crack. Walker hadn't finished the cut, but he'd cut enough. The narrowed section of the trunk exploded into splinters and dust, and the tree headed for Janaina.

Her heart went into overdrive and she rolled to the side.

The tree came crashing down. It hit the other two as planned and all three headed for the ground.

But as they fell, a branch sheared from the first tree. The sharpened tip plunged for the ground like a dagger. Walker looked up. His eyes went wide in terror, glowing white against the bright red blood coating his face. He screamed. The branch impaled him straight through the mouth and pinned his head to the ground. His body jerked once and then went still. The light left his eyes.

The three trees continued their fall. To Janaina, it seemed like slow motion. She prayed they would miss their target, but Walker's aim had been horrifically true. The three fell across the pyramid opening. Loose stones were the first to tumble, and she held out faint hope that that would be all. But the impact was too much, and the pyramid's side collapsed in a cascade of huge stone blocks and gray dust.

The snake would never squeeze its way out of there.

But neither would Grant.

CHAPTER THIRTY-THREE

The pyramid tunnel was pitch black.

With the snake approaching, Grant had bolted into the dark tube, hoping that the right turn meant that he was heading back to the entrance passage. Unable to see a thing, he moved as quickly as his injured ankle allowed along the wall, feeling his way sideways and with his other hand outstretched forward. Just as he was about to despair that he was in some kind of maze, he felt air flowing from up ahead. It had to be from the entrance.

Then the structure shook. A force like an earthquake moved blocks that had to weigh hundreds of pounds. Ground stone sifted down from every crevice. The pyramid moaned.

Then came a thundering crash like an avalanche in an echo chamber. A gritty blast of humid air blew over Grant from up the tunnel. He covered his mouth and nose with his shirt. Sandy dust coated his skin. He worked his way forward along the tunnel wall.

He stepped forward with his bad foot and hit something hard. He hissed a profanity. He knelt and felt around in front of him. A pile of broken stone filled the tunnel. The flow of fresh air had stopped.

Something had gone wrong outside. The trees must have dropped early and collapsed the pyramid. The trap-the-snake part of the plan had worked. The get-Grant-out-alive part had failed. Miserably.

Grant broke out in a cold sweat. This exit route was blocked. If the trees had done their job, and it sure as hell looked like they did, the main corridor wasn't going to be any better. And if this pyramid had any emergency exits, the Viper King would have used one, instead of dying here and letting Grant use his skull as a gong hammer.

With no way forward, he'd have to go back. And there was a major snake waiting for him at the tunnel's end. Worse, it might come exploring up this tunnel before Grant got out of it. The idea of being devoured in the dark was somehow much worse than dying in the dim light of the sacrifice room. He hobbled a little faster down the tunnel. Soon the dusky light of the main chamber lit the exit.

He reached the tunnel's end. He took a deep breath and looked around the edge. The light wasn't great, but it was good enough to confirm that there wasn't a giant snake blocking his exit. He stuck his head further out.

The area around the altar was clear save for the bones of the dead men. Strangler fig vines over the snake statue still oscillated from the force of the collapse. A few cracked blocks from the pyramid sides lay on the floor. The room had not collapsed, but he sure wouldn't call it safe. He looked around to the left and froze.

The snake lay sticking just out of the corridor entrance. Rubble buried the back two-thirds. Its head lay at a cocked angle against a fallen stone. Blood seeped from a gash near its closed eyes.

"I'll be damned," Grant said. "Something finally broke my way."

A dead snake eliminated one of two problems. Of course the remaining problem was escaping an inescapable prison.

He limped around to the rear of the altar. There were other tunnels, other passages. The collapse had sealed this one, but maybe it opened others. He didn't need much of an opening, maybe a foot wide.

He looked down at his gut.

Okay, two feet wide, he thought.

He shuffled past the stone snake's tail. The Viper King's crowned head lay beside it.

"Thanks for getting me into this mess," he said to the skull.

Grant stepped on a human femur. It rolled and he teetered backward. His foot shot out and booted the Viper King's skull. It sailed away from the altar and hit the Aztec gong. The metal rang and reverberated through the room.

The great snake hissed.

Grant's heart skipped a beat. He grabbed the stone serpent's tail and pulled himself up to see over the altar. The giant snake's yellow slit eyes were wide open.

The snake slithered forward. Broken stone blocks slid off the scales on its back. A low rumble rolled up from the corridor's far end as the pyramid debris collapsed behind the advancing snake. It headed straight for the altar.

Grant thought fast. The tunnels were traps, all dead ends. The bones scattered around him proved there wasn't any secret passage under the floor. With this screwed up ankle, he sure wasn't going to outrun the snake.

He looked up. Hazy light shined in through the narrow slits at the pyramid's peak. The collapse of the entrance had widened some. Strangler fig vines hung down from the openings, stopping a meter over the serpent statue's head. Grant rationalized he could squeeze through the enlarged opening and the awful idea of climbing out of here took shape.

The snake hissed. The stink of Rafael's digesting corpse filled the air. Grant needed no further encouragement.

He grabbed the statue's tail and climbed up the ridge along its back. Every step on his injured foot sent a spear of pain up through his leg. But he was moving so fast there wasn't time to baby that ankle.

The snake was less than a meter from the altar. Grant climbed up over the stone altar, almost to the statue's head.

The snake coiled, aimed at Grant, and struck.

It jerked to a stop short of its target. The fallen stones had held the last part of the snake in the tunnel. It twisted back in fury to see what had kept it from its prize.

Grant scrambled to the top of the snake statue. The vines waved just out of reach.

The snake dove at the pile of rubble that pinned it in place. It used its triangular head like a plow and bulldozed the stone from around its body. Its tail whipped free, arced across the room and turned a swath of Aztec bones into dust. It snapped against the altar base like cracking a whip. The snake spun its head toward Grant and its eyes narrowed.

He was out of time.

He couldn't reach the vines. He rose and stood on the statue's head. His burning ankle threatened to collapse. He crouched, prayed, and jumped.

His right hand caught a vine. His left hand caught nothing. He clamped his hand around the vine, but his weight was too much, and the rough bark began to run through his grip.

He clamped his other hand to the vine and wrapped his legs around the bottom. With strength fueled by adrenalin, he climbed.

The snake launched itself at Grant. Or at where he had been. It crashed into the statue's head and turned it into rubble and dust. Scales scraped Grant's feet as the snake barreled by underneath him.

The snake hissed in raging fury at the loss of its prey. It hit the ground and with a snap of its body sent more Aztec bones flying. It coiled for another strike and snicked out its forked tongue to taste the air.

Grant's arms and shoulders burned so hot he thought his shirt would catch fire. He pulled and shimmied his way up the vine. The vine shifted against the rocks overhead and sent a cascade of pebbles and sand down on his head. Freedom was impossibly far away.

The snake launched itself at Grant. He grabbed an adjacent vine and pulled. He swung right. The snake sailed past him. It crashed into the statue of itself. The head sheared off, dropped on the altar, and shattered. Then the altar cracked down the center and collapsed. Unsupported, the rest of the snake statue dropped to the floor.

Momentum kept the snake flying forward toward the metal plate. The snake twisted its head just enough that the side of its body took the impact. The enormous gong bellowed a deep tone on impact, and then broke in half. The bottom section crashed to the floor and the snake dropped on top of it. The top half bounced against the wall. A jagged edge ran along the bottom.

Grant looked down. Big mistake. He hung a dozen meters over the rubble of the statue and altar. If the fall didn't kill him, the snake would. And his arms screamed that they were completely done with this Tarzan routine.

Looking up was depressing, looking down was terrifying. He looked straight ahead. Below him the snake hissed and the sound of grinding stone told him it was repositioning for another attack. He gritted his teeth, and pulled himself upwards.

Hand over hand, he inched his way up the vine. With each tug he rocked the ropy bark against the stone's edge at the pyramid's peak. He doubted it would take long to saw it in half.

Sweat poured down his back. His slick palms threatened to slide down the vine if he gave his effort the slightest slack. Each pull upward moved him an increasingly shorter distance up, as his muscles grew too tired to pull as far as the time before.

The snake whipped its tail across the room and sent loose stone flying against the wall. Grant dared a glance down. The snake lay in a coil beneath him.

Panic-induced energy surged through him. He pulled hand-over-hand so fast the vine rocked back and forth with each reach.

The snake opened its mouth wide and attacked. Like the release of a spring, it shot straight up. But Grant's swing on the vine moved him left. The great fangs passed him, missing by centimeters.

The snake's head snapped to the side. A broadside of scales struck Grant across the back. With a death grip on the vine, he flew into the pyramid wall. His head struck stone. The vertebrae in his neck crackled like popcorn.

The snake fell. It landed across the broken altar. Its head dropped across the broken half of the metal plate.

Grant swung back across the room, headed for one of the two rusting mounts that held the hanging half of the great plate suspended. His head felt like it had been smacked with a hammer. He brought his eyes into focus and saw the mount in the wall. A million-to-one-shot came to mind.

He brought his body into an L and aimed his feet at the ancient metal. His weight finally worked in his favor as his boots smashed into the rusting mount. It cracked, then disintegrated. That side of the gong dropped.

The full weight of the great gong fell on the remaining chain and mount. The chain snapped with the sound of a rifle shot.

The enormous plate dropped down like a guillotine's blade. The jagged edge found its mark just below the snake's head. It dug in and released a spray of thick, red blood. The snake writhed with a furious hiss. Then it dropped to the ground and did not move.

Grant's vine pulled him back to the center of the room. He had been fooled once before into thinking the snake was dead, and no matter what he saw, he wasn't going down that road again. He resumed his climb, with regular, quick looks over his shoulder.

He covered the last few meters at a snail's pace. But finally he reached up and grabbed the edge of the stone around the pyramid opening. He gripped the other side with his other hand, and pulled. The opening was narrower than he'd thought. His arms felt like they had nothing left to give, but somehow he mustered one last bit of strength. He pulled himself up and wedged his shoulders through the open space. His head popped out into blessedly fresh air, tinged with the scent of the orchids around the pyramid's base.

He wriggled forward, and then his gut wedged him in tight. His arms were spent, his legs hung down useless on the other side, kicking at air.

He tried to scream for help. Nothing came out but a squeak. Too much exertion, too little water.

Overhead, a vulture made a lazy circle over the pyramid's peak.

"If after all that, I die up here," he rasped to himself, "I'm going to be very pissed."

CHAPTER THIRTY-FOUR

From this uncomfortable vantage point, Grant could look down the crumbled side of the pyramid. The trees had certainly done their work well. The trunks lay half-buried in the rubble. He was right in thinking he'd never have gotten out that way.

At the base, Janaina stood beside a stand of orchids. He couldn't see Walker anywhere. Embarrassing as it was going to be, she'd have to help pull him out of this mess.

Again he tried to summon a shout. Out came a gravelly wheeze. All Janaina's focus was on the ruined side, no doubt wondering if there was still a way in or out. Half a rotund paleontologist sticking out of the wall wouldn't attract much attention. She wasn't going to look up to the pyramid's peak unless he made her. He was going to have to send a message.

A few broken blocks lay on the level in front of him. He stretched out and grabbed the closest one. With an awkward pre-schooler's toss, he lobbed the piece of rock down the pyramid side toward Janaina. It hit one step in the pyramid, bounced to the next, then wedged itself against one of the collapsed blocks.

"Damnit."

He stretched out further. Tendons in his shoulder popped. His fingertips grazed a larger chunk of rock. He flicked it closer and then grabbed it. This one had some heft to it.

He took a deep breath and lobbed it harder down the pyramid's side.

The stone hit the first step with a crack. It bounced high and hit the second. Gravity started to earn its keep and the rock accelerated. This one looked destined to actually reach the ground. Grant smiled.

At the third step the stone hit another bit of rubble. A second stone pinged off a block to the side and joined the first on its downward path.

On its next bounce, it nudged a third off an edge, just as the first stone hit the next block with enough force to send cracks across the top, and a miniature landslide of stones down the face.

Grant's face fell.

Soon a tiny avalanche of tumbling rocks bounced down the pyramid's side. The further it traveled, the larger the recruits to the cause grew. And Grant had perfectly aimed the rolling mass at Janaina.

He squeaked out a warning even he could barely hear. The rockslide was halfway down the pyramid.

One smaller stone bounced hard and high, breaking away from the pack like a Triple Crown winner. It bounced on a step and then hit the ground at Janaina's feet.

She looked up and saw the onrushing crush of rock and dust. Her jaw went slack.

She bolted to the left. The avalanche rolled down and bounced to a stop right where she'd been standing. Janaina exhaled in relief and looked up the side of the pyramid. Her eyes locked on Grant, first in shock, then with elation.

He managed a sheepish little wave.

She pounced on the pyramid and scrambled up the undamaged side. She reached him with a big smile on her face. "You made it out!"

"Well, halfway," he said in a dry, raspy voice. "I'm going to need some help."

"You are like Winnie the Pooh, stuck in the tree trunk."

"Thanks for that flattering reference. Now get to work, Piglet."

Janaina dropped her pack and loosened one of the stones around the opening. Then she grabbed Grant's hands and pulled. Grant sucked in his stomach and wiggled back and forth. Centimeter by centimeter, he slid forward. His waist passed through the opening and he flopped down on the pyramid step. He and Janaina collapsed side by side. Janaina pulled a water bottle from her sack and gave it to Grant. He downed the contents in an instant. Even hot, the water felt rejuvenating.

"Thank you," he said. "I thought I was going to be stuck in there forever."

"There was a cascade of stones a moment ago. You were lucky to be above it."

Grant felt his face redden. "Yes, very lucky. Where's Walker?"

Janaina pointed to one of the felled trees. "Killed by a falling branch. Served him right for trapping you in there."

"He cut the trees down early on purpose?"

"He said he'd stolen emeralds from the pyramid, and would kill both of us before he went back to be rich."

Grant remembered the missing emeralds from the serpent statue's eyes. "And I thought Marcos was the untrustworthy one."

"He was. They were in it together. They ran the logging crew just to find the pyramid." She stuck her head into the opening in the pyramid's peak and looked down into the dim central room. "The giant snake?"

"Dead. It won't be breaking out."

Janaina gave him a sideways look. "You killed the giant snake?"

"You say that like you doubt my monster-slaying skills."

"I have seen you in action."

"Let's just agree that it is dead, I was there when it died, and it was the culmination of my master escape plan. And we'll leave it at that."

"I'm sure it will be quite heroic when you put it in your next novel."

"You have no idea."

They both looked out across the rainforest. The smoke from the burning barricade had calmed down to a few dark wisps.

"We still need to get home," Janaina said.

"The canoe we arrived in is still at the camp. We can get downriver, maybe catch the Cruz do Sul relief boat on its way up. Worst case, we paddle down to the Atlantic Ocean. We can't stay here. There's still that spider infestation."

"Spiders we must get past to get to that canoe."

"We've made it through worse."

Janaina smiled and laughed. "Sadly, that may be true."

She stood up, offered her hand, and helped Grant up. Every muscle in his body ranted in protest. "Forget the three-day shower plan. I'm moving into a heated whirlpool when I get home."

Step by step, they worked their way down the pyramid side. Grant tried to favor his good ankle, and hobbled off-balance.

"You are hurt?" Janaina said.

"I sprained my ankle. Nothing permanent, but running out of this rainforest isn't an option."

Just as they reached the ground, Emiliano burst from the tree line, green blood-stained machete in hand. He staggered to them. His chest heaved as he tried to catch his breath. Dripping sweat had drawn lines through the smoke smudge that covered his face and arms. He seemed on the verge of collapse as he spoke.

"The spiders," he said. "They are coming."

THE CURSE OF THE VIPER KING

CHAPTER THIRTY-FIVE

"How many spiders?" Grant said.

"Too many," Emiliano said. "The barricade collapsed. They all attacked."

Janaina looked back at the tree line. "Who else escaped?"

Emiliano just looked at the ground and shook his head.

"Three of us against an arachnid army," Grant said. "A dream come true."

"I think you mean nightmare," Janaina said.

"Sarcasm voice on that one," Grant said.

Grant realized they had nothing to battle the spiders. He limped over to Walker's corpse. Flies buzzed around his mouth where the branch had impaled him. Janaina was correct, it served him right.

"Remember this next time you try to seal someone in a pyramid," Grant said. He fought the urge to give the body a kick.

The falling tree had crushed the chainsaw, but Walker still had his machete in his belt. Grant slid it out. He remembered how little good the blade did in the last spider encounter.

"Where's the rifle?" he asked.

"I could not find it," Janaina said. "It must be under the tree."

"Machetes aren't going to be enough," he said.

Emiliano raised a finger. "The orchids. They are spider poison. It makes them burn. Rub flowers on the blades, on your body. It is how I survived."

"Orchids are not poison," Janaina said.

"Not to us," Grant answered. "But to creatures that stopped evolving before orchids did, they very well could be. Might have even been one of their extinction's root causes. No pun intended."

"It would explain the spiders' fear of the wall," Janaina said.

"And why there are so many growing around the pyramid. Feral descendants of ones likely cultivated as a form of defense."

The three went to the orchids, plucked the flowers and crushed them against their machetes and all over their bodies.

"This is the best I've smelled in weeks," Grant said.

Janaina finished and went back to Walker's corpse. She searched his pockets and found the two massive emeralds. "These were all he really cared about." She looked at the sealed pyramid opening. "They cannot go back inside. They will go in a museum. I know trustworthy contacts."

"Another reason to get home alive," Grant said. "Like we need one."

Grant picked up his pack from where he'd left it before entering the pyramid. He passed Walker's pack to Emiliano. "Let's get out of here."

Emiliano headed back into the jungle and Grant and Janaina followed. Grant slowed them up considerably with his limping walk and he feared he might get all of them killed. The narrow path they took seemed ripe to host a spider ambush. Grant's heart wouldn't stop thudding. Every leaf rustle and every twig snap threatened to announce the arrival of their eight-legged doom.

After an adrenaline-fuelled eternity, they neared the jungle's edge without any signs of spiders. Grant guessed that the arachnids preferred the open area near the fence to being cramped between jungle trees and bushes.

The three emerged where the group had spent the night. The area looked like a war zone. Bodies lay all across the clearing, most webbed and desiccated. The charred remains of the barricade lay in a smoldering line across the opening in the fence. One spider stood guard far off on their side of the wall, near a burned out hole in the ground.

The three ducked down behind some palms.

"I only see one spider," Emiliano said. "By where Bruno burned out the nest. That's what sent them up over the barricade."

"One spider, three of us," Grant said. "Better odds than I was counting on."

"Still not good," Janaina said.

"But they'll never be better."

"The barricade will be cool enough now that we can cross it," Emiliano said.

Grant looked at the dozens of meters between them and the wall, and then the gap beyond that to the relative safety of the jungle. "Look, I can't make a run for it with this ankle. But you two can. That spider isn't facing us. Run for it and it won't even see you. If it attacks there are two of you, all slathered in orchids. You can fight it off."

"What about you?" Janaina said.

"The grass is pretty deep. I'm going to crawl. I'll be well out of sight. It will take a while. I'll catch up with you at the camp."

"Certainly not," Janaina said. "Even with the orchid oils you can't hold off a spider if it sees you. Especially not with that ankle."

"One crawls, we all crawl," Emiliano said. "We are stronger together."

Janaina nodded in agreement.

"This is where I tell you to save yourself," Grant said to Janaina, "and you don't pay any attention, right?"

"You are correct."

"Okay, then let's get crawling."

Emiliano dropped to all fours and began a beeline through the grass to the opening in the wall. Janaina followed in the trail he compressed in the grass. Grant brought up the rear.

The grass had caught the scent of the barricade's blaze, and the stink of charred wood fought with the sweet scent of the crushed orchids. A reminder of death mingled with a promise of life.

Every crunch of the grass beneath Grant's palms seemed bullhorn-loud, certain to bring the spider sentinel running to investigate. But he dared not peek above the grasses, fearing that if the sound of his progress hadn't alerted the spider, the sight of his head above the green grass tips certainly would. He kept his eyes to the ground, trying to land his hands and knees in the same impressions left by the two before him.

Ahead of him Janaina stopped. He almost ran into her butt. Emiliano had stopped in front of her. Emiliano veered left and continued on. Janaina followed his path. When Grant made it to the spot where Emiliano had paused, he saw why.

One of the loggers lay dead in the grass. A clot of webbing bound his feet together from the knees down. His gray skin lay shrunken tight to his skull, even his eyes were deflated. White teeth glowed in the sunlight from a mouth permanently frozen open in terror.

Grant continued on.

Soon he began to pass bits of charred branches, the remnants of the exploded barricade. The tangy smell of burned wood smothered all others. In a moment they paused again, this time side-by-side. Just ahead, the grass had been burned down to dusky nubs. Beyond it, the black, skeletal remains of the barricade framed the opening in the wall, their doorway to freedom, ten meters away.

Grant dared a peek above the grass tips. The sole spider had wandered over to the tree line behind them, further from the opening in the wall.

Emiliano looked at Grant. "Ready?"

"Are you kidding? Ready for a triathlon."

Janaina rolled her eyes.

"Let's go," Grant said. "Quick and quiet."

The three stood and began a dash for the exit. Grant tried to keep up. He fought through the pain and pounded his blaring ankle with every stride. If he lived through this, he'd have a long canoe trip to nurse his injury.

They made it to the barricade debris. Curls of smoke still rose from some of the larger logs. Emiliano darted around them and the smoke swirled after him, as if trying to reach out and hold him back. Janaina matched his steps. Grant fell behind.

From the tree line came a spider's high-pitched growl. The sentinel had seen them and charged.

"Hurry!" Grant said.

They crossed through the opening and stopped dead.

Three more spiders blocked their path.

CHAPTER THIRTY-SIX

The three spiders spread their mandibles and growled. Saliva dripped from their fangs. The middle spider's eyes locked on Janaina. She sensed blind, uncontrolled fury.

Grant whirled to face the spider charging from the rear. Emiliano and Janaina pivoted and the three of them stood almost shoulder to shoulder in a circle, machetes out, ready to face the attack from all angles.

Janaina knew there was no way they'd survive. A few well-placed web balls would immobilize them, if the spiders even bothered. Four on three was more than enough advantage, and who knows how many more were waiting behind these. The three of them couldn't swing the poisoned blades fast enough to stay alive.

The two spiders on the ends charged. The center spider spit a web ball aimed at Janaina's head. It rocketed at her with incredible speed. She ducked just in time for the ball to whiz past her head. It struck Grant on the shoulder and spun him to the ground.

The single spider on their side of the wall saw its chance. It launched itself toward the three.

One of the other charging spiders flashed at the edge of her vision. Janaina whirled to face it.

The third spider was just meters away from Emiliano, coming fast enough to flatten him.

Grant rose to one knee, machete half-raised in a hopeless defense.

Janaina's heart hammered. Her fight-or-flight response demanded an answer. She opted to go out swinging. She brandished her blade, screamed, and charged the closest spider.

A sound like a chorus of flutes infused the air.

The spiders stopped dead in their tracks.

Janaina couldn't. A combination of momentum and panic for self-preservation kept her driving forward. All that registered was burying her blade between the spider's black, lifeless eyes. She passed through the opening in the barrier fence.

A man stepped out in front of her. He was her height, but twice her weight, and every ounce of it was muscle. He wore just a loincloth with a gourd covering his penis. His skin was slathered with hand-applied swirls of white paint. He reached up and grabbed the wrist of her hand that held the machete. He pulled her down and her own momentum drove her onto the ground. She hit the earth between the spider's front legs and nearly under its mouth. The man drove a knee into her back.

Two others stepped out before Grant and Emiliano. The painted men just stood like ghosts between the two and the now-still spiders.

Emiliano checked Grant and Janaina over his shoulders. Grant stood up, breathing hard. He looked past the man in the body paint to the spider.

"Thank God," Grant said. "This sport has needed referees for about two days."

The flute song sounded again. The four spiders turned south. The three outside the enclosure passed though the opening, joined the one on the inside, and the four moved off along the inside of the wall. The man who pinned Janaina to the ground helped her up.

A woman with a shaved head stepped out from behind the wall. Unnaturally tall, she also wore the same white paint over her body. But she wore a knee length skirt of white crocodile hide and a similar swath of material across her chest. In one hand she held a lute-like instrument made from three different diameters of bamboo with holes drilled up along the shafts.

On the center of her forehead was painted a black oval. From each side, a line traced the contour of her eyebrow, then hooked around her eye, in the shape of a spider's leg.

"You are safe now," she said in accented Portuguese.

"You speak Portuguese?" Janaina said.

"And English," she said to Grant. "We've had centuries to learn other tongues. I am Citlali, Chief Protector of the Kingdom."

"We appreciate you saving our lives," Grant said.

Citlali's eyes narrowed. "Yet we do not appreciate you trespassing, destroying that which is not yours, releasing those we have kept safely imprisoned."

"None of that was our idea," Grant said. "Marcos did all that, and he died for doing it."

"As did many others," Janaina added.

"I weep for none of you. The punishment fits the crime."

Grant pointed in the direction the spiders retreated. "You control the spiders?"

"To an extent, as much as any wild animal can be controlled. They will not stay calm for long. Come."

She beckoned them forward, beyond the orchid wall. As soon as they stepped out, a dozen natives appeared, all slathered in white, carrying logs and branches. They set to work closing the gap in the wall. A line of women exited the jungle, each carrying an orchid rooted in a ball of earth.

"Your people maintain the wall and keep the spiders inside," Janaina said. "And keep the orchids blooming."

"A floral electric fence," Grant said.

"As we have for generations," Citlali said. "When King Axayacatl conquered the Viper King, he sealed the vanquished within the pyramid, a feast for the evil creature the Viper King had raised. But the spider army was another matter. Hundreds would have died exterminating them. They stayed near the pyramid, so the great king trained my ancestors in the Viper King's ways to control the creatures. We played to them night and day to keep them docile until the orchid wall could be finished. Then all the evil the Viper King had set loose on the world had been imprisoned.

"But a prison needs guards. My family was entrusted with a company of the great king's most valiant soldiers, and given the task of keeping the Aztec Empire safe from these creatures. We used the orchids to reinforce the walls, and coated ourselves in their paste to protect ourselves when we knew we would encounter the spiders. For hundreds of years we have maintained the wall, kept the areas around it clear, and kept the demons of the Viper King locked away."

Citlali's face twisted in anger. "Until now. You cut away our forest. You freed the spiders. You destroyed the pyramid. Generations of work undone by idiots in search of dark wood."

"When you say it that way," Grant said, "you make it sound like a bad thing."

Janaina's eyes narrowed at Grant. This was no time for his sarcasm voice.

"Only two of our party trespassed," Janaina said. "The rest of us only came here running for our lives. Just three of us remain. Emiliano has lost his brother. Grant and I are not of this group. We stumbled upon them as we were lost in the rainforest. He is thousands of miles from home and missing his wife."

Grant started to open his mouth to object. Janaina sent him a withering look that locked his jaw half-open.

"We tried to help you," Citlali said. She pointed to Emiliano. "We returned this one to you instead of leaving him to die in the jungle from a spider attack."

Janaina remembered Emiliano's memory lapse about how he'd gotten back to camp, and the smudges of white where the Aztec descendants had grabbed his shoulders to carry him.

"But you did not leave," Citlali said with anger. "Instead you pushed into the rainforest and just made things worse."

"Wait," Grant said. "All the orchids around us when we woke up…"

"Another layer of protection for you, in case one spider had stayed behind. We had the spiders under control to allow you to depart. And then you destroyed the nursery and there was no stopping them."

"That was the act of one man," Emiliano said. "And he is dead."

"That is no consolation. And worse will come when you go downriver and tell the world what happened here. Outsiders will arrive like ants by the thousands. All will be lost forever."

"My job," Janaina said, "my passion, is working to protect people like you, the native peoples who still live here as their ancestors have. I will say nothing of anything here."

She turned and gave Grant a "Well, your turn!" look.

"I study the bones of giant creatures, dead for millions of years," Grant said. "I've had enough of fighting live ones. All I want to do is get back home to my classroom."

Janaina raised an eyebrow at him.

Grant gritted his teeth. "And to my wife."

Citlali looked unmoved. "The risk is too great."

"I will stay in their place," Emiliano said.

"What?" Janaina and Grant said together.

"I will stay and help fix what we damaged. The wall. The pyramid. I'll know the ways of anyone from the outside world who stumbles upon us again. I'll help your people redirect them and stay hidden."

"You can't stay out here," Grant said.

"Why not? My brother is dead, and he was the last of my family. I have no money, now I have no job, and rarely did before this one. I leave nothing behind. I owe this woman for saving my life. I need to pay that back. And I need a purpose."

Citlali stared Emiliano down as she contemplated his offer. Then she looked at Grant and shook her head, as if dismissing the idea.

"I know the officials who protect the land," Janaina pleaded, "who keep some of it safe from outsiders. I know all the ways to keep this area undisturbed. No one will come back. No more of your forest will fall."

Citlali turned to Emiliano. "Life here is not easy."

"Life in a barrio is worse."

"Very well," Citlali said. "You two go. Do not come back. Make certain no one else does. Next time we will not stay hidden. These descendants of great warriors are great warriors still. We will drive you off."

"You have my promise," Janaina said.

"And mine," Grant added.

"Go before I change my mind."

"Emiliano," Janaina said, "you are certain?"

"More than in a very long time."

"I do not have Gabriel's star. I had to use it to stop Walker. I'm so sorry."

"Gabriel would be happy with that. And he will live inside me forever, star or no star."

She touched his shoulder in farewell, then she and Grant turned to head back to the logging camp. Then she remembered something.

She pulled the snake statue's two emerald eyes from her pocket. She handed them to Citlali.

"One of the men stole these to make himself rich," Janaina said. "I was going to put them in a museum. They cannot go back where they were, but they should stay where they are."

Citlali stared at the two jewels as they sparkled in her hand. "I have never been in the sealed pyramid. No one has. But my parents told the story passed down from the start of our time here. A story of a great snake statue with emerald eyes that sat at the pyramid's center, surrounded by death."

"The story was true."

"So I will tell my children. And they will tell theirs."

Janaina nodded, then she and Grant headed for the jungle trail that would restart their journey home.

CHAPTER THIRTY-SEVEN

Grant stepped out of the clearing and back onto the jungle trail to the camp. He sighed with relief.

"This trail scared the hell out of me when we followed it in," he said. "Now it's a blessing to be back on it."

Janaina slapped him on the back of the head. "What was your smart comments back there? Not the time for sarcastic voice!"

The slap stung. "Yeah, sorry. Sometimes things slip out before I even know I thought them."

"Next time, I will let your mouth make you into spider food."

In a while they arrived back at the camp. With none of the work crew there, it seemed hollow, haunted. A shiver ran up Grant's spine.

"Now we need to get home," Janaina said.

"We still have the canoe."

"The canoe barely floats."

"But 'barely' is still better than 'sunken'," Grant said.

They headed down to the river, past Walker's house. He had pulled the canoe up into the trees near the water's edge. They turned past the corner of the house and stopped. The canoe was out in the sun.

"Someone moved the canoe," Grant said.

"The same person who will be taking it downstream," a voice said behind them.

They spun around to see Marcos standing in the shadow of the building. His left arm hung bloody and limp at his side. He held Walker's rifle in his right, pointed at them. Grant and Janaina raised their hands.

"Marcos," Grant deadpanned. "Thank heaven you're alive."

"We thought the snake killed you," Janaina said.

"The verb you are looking for there is 'hoped'," Grant said.

"Shut up, American." Marcos turned to Janaina. "The snake almost killed me. I wedged myself back into a crevice between broken stones. I thought I was going to starve to death like that. But then you arrived, drew it outside the pyramid. I was on my way out when I met Walker coming in. We pried out the emeralds together. The plan was for him to let the snake kill both of you. Then we'd both head downstream and get rich."

"And you abandoned him," Grant said.

"Only after he was dead. I liberated his rifle, and decided to let the spiders finish all of you."

"Well, your plan failed," Janaina said. "We are alive and the emeralds are still deep in the jungle where they belong."

"Just like I had my own escape route around the spiders at the opening in the wall, I have my own treasure to cash in." He tapped the butt of the rifle against a big bulge that hung heavy in his right cargo pocket. "I learned a long time ago to always take care of myself first."

Grant's initial dislike for the man, which had morphed into loathing, now exploded into raging hatred.

"Now slowly drop the machetes to the ground," Marcos said.

Grant entertained the thought of throwing his blade and having it impale the little thieving bastard, but he was certain that kind of stunt only worked in movies. He and Janaina laid down the machetes.

"Now, I was having a hard time with the canoe, one-handed and all. You two pull it down to the river."

Janaina looked at Grant.

"He's got the gun," Grant said.

Grant hobbled over and grabbed the stern of the canoe. Janaina took the bow. The paddle was still tucked inside. They walked it down to the river in a jerky fashion as Grant nursed his bad ankle. Janaina put the bow in the water. Grant pushed it halfway in and held onto the stern. Marcos waved Janaina away with the rifle barrel and she walked back along the river bank. Keeping the rifle pointed at Grant, Marcos made his way down to the canoe. He stepped ankle deep into the water, then gingerly into the canoe. He sat facing Grant.

"Now give me a push," he said.

"How about a roll?"

"How about a bullet in the brain?"

Grant dug in and gave the canoe a big push. It knifed out into the water and caught the current right away. Marcos broke into a big smile. He shouted back to shore.

"The funniest part?" He waved the rifle at them. "No bullets!"

"Not the funniest part," Grant shouted back.

He held up the two belts he'd banded the cracked canoe together with before they landed at the logging camp. Marcos looked confused.

Then the stern of the canoe creaked and dipped lower in the river. Marcos looked into the canoe bottom and panic filled his eyes. He turned the rifle around and flailed at the rising water with the butt, trying to bail the doomed boat. But as the current pulled the canoe further and faster out and downstream, the stern sank lower. Then in an instant, it and Marcos were gone.

Marcos' head popped up from the dark river water. He gulped the air and sank back under. With a pocket full of metal and only one working arm, he could not win this match against the mighty Amazon. One hand broke the surface, then slipped back under the swirling water. A stream of bubbles burst in the water, and were carried downstream.

Janaina ran over and gave Grant a hug. "That was brilliant! You barbequed his goose."

Grant cut himself off from correcting her. "But now we have no way home."

He looked around the compound. A pile of logs stood stacked by the broken barge.

"Walker said men had built rafts and floated downstream to get home," Grant said. "We just need to lash some of that together."

The two of them rolled a few of the smaller logs over to the water. Using some of the rope by the pile, they lashed several together into a pretty loose raft. The pushed it into the river and it did indeed float. Janaina went back and returned with two two-by-fours for paddles.

"Good enough for Tom Sawyer, good enough for us," Grant said.

They packed some food, cast off, and began to travel where the current would take them. Preferably home.

CHAPTER THIRTY-EIGHT

They'd been on the river hours and the sun was on its way down. The raft barely floated with their weight on it and was awash with each ripple in the river.

"So do we try to run this thing aground overnight?" Grant said.

"Do you want to share your sleeping with jungle animals?"

"Not really."

"Then I say we keep floating. There are no falls and the river grows wider and slower the further we travel."

"Maybe we will wake up in civilization."

"With a dream of triple cheeseburgers?"

"And a mountain of fries."

"Will this adventure become another book?"

Grant scratched his chin. "I don't know. Maybe two. One about fighting monsters in the clouds, another with the brave hero battling the curse of the Viper King."

"Does the story get a heroine as well, a woman struggling for the rights of indigenous peoples?"

"Maybe. The hero has to save *somebody*."

Janaina scooped a handful of water and splashed him with it.

They floated around a hairpin curve in the river. Downstream, a squat red and white boat chugged toward them, towing a barge like the one wrecked at the logging camp. Grant's pulse soared. He sat up on the raft.

"Yes! Rescue!"

Janaina smiled and turned around to see the boat. Her face fell.

"This is the Cruz do Sul boat," she said.

"Just who we expected, on its way to the logging camp."

"Walker and his crew were contractors, they did not recognize me. This is a corporate crew. They will know I am the anti-logger who cost them millions."

"Even if they do, they can't not rescue us."

"They will want to go to the camp. They will see it is abandoned, the barge destroyed. Everything damaged. We are going to tell them it was attacked by giant spiders?"

"No, I hadn't planned on ever telling anyone that. We'll say we were never there."

"Yes, we will tell them they found an environmentalist downstream of a destroyed logging camp and that was all a coincidence. If anyone on the boat knew someone working at the camp, we will never get off that ship alive."

Grant had to admit she had a point, no one would believe the truth. And they'd promised Citlali not to tell the truth anyway. This rescue wasn't going to end up being a rescue after all.

"Paddle closer to shore," Grant said. "We'll pull into the shadows, hide until they pass."

They both grabbed two-by-fours and began to paddle.

They hadn't tried propelling the raft before, they'd just floated with the current. It was immediately obvious that they had no control. The two-by-fours were too small, the raft too balky. They did a lot of splashing but no propelling.

Someone on the bow of the boat shouted. A horn blasted.

They'd been spotted. The ship adjusted course to intercept them.

"With all we've been through," Grant said, "it can't end like this."

Behind them, an engine roared. Around the bend in the river came a river cruise ship, bright white, twenty meters long and three stories high, perched on what looked like two giant kayaks. Slatted shutters covered the sides, most of them propped open. Light and music spilled from every one.

"What the hell is that?" Grant said.

"River cruise!" Janaina said. "Rich people pretending they are roughing it."

People on the bow shouted a warning as they saw the raft just a hundred meters ahead. The ship's horn sounded and the engines shifted into reverse.

Crewmen dropped a rope ladder over the side. The pilot nudged the boat up alongside the raft. The wake sloshed over Grant and soaked him to the chest. He still smiled.

The Cruz do Sul boat chugged by on the cruise ship's far side and continued upstream.

Grant helped Janaina up the ladder first. He followed and when he got to the top he collapsed on the deck, thrilled to be on something dry and solid.

A middle-aged man's broad head leaned in and blocked his field of view. He had gaps in his teeth and wore a New York Yankees baseball hat. Wonder filled his eyes.

"Damn, dude, you look like you've been on the wrong end of an adventure."

"You have no idea," Grant said.

CHAPTER THIRTY-NINE

Six months later.

Grant looked out at the lecture hall. Most of the seats were empty, even though his class on the Triassic Era had almost a hundred students. He could not fault the missing. It was Friday afternoon before the Thanksgiving break. He loved to teach and even he wouldn't have been here if he hadn't had to. A perfect, crisp fall day was going to waste on the other side of the windows.

"So at about 199 million years ago," Grant said, pointing a red laser at a map on the screen behind him, "tectonic forces finally won out, and began to split the supercontinent Pangea into Laurasia in the north and Gondwana in the south."

He checked the clock on the podium.

"And that's a good stopping point for today. If you don't mind getting cheated on your tuition money, I'll call this class over fifteen minutes early."

Books slammed, chairs scraped, phones dinged. The lecture hall emptied in two seconds. Grant gathered his notes.

A man in a business suit approached down the main aisle. He carried a thin messenger bag. He had a sharp haircut and wire rim glasses. He stopped in front of the podium.

"Professor Coleman? I'm Matt Calloway."

He held out his hand. Grant didn't shake it.

"If you are a new lawyer representing my ex-wife, I'm all paid up."

He smiled. "No, I'm afraid I have to admit I'm a lawyer, but I'm not representing your ex-wife. I'm representing the estate of Professor Maxwell Carson."

Grant caught his breath. He gave the man's hand a slow shake. "Professor Carson is dead?"

"Well, that's why I'm here. You studied under him throughout your doctoral classes?"

"Yes, he was inspirational. I literally owe my career choice to him."

"This summer, he was doing field research in China."

"At his age? He has to be seventy."

"Seventy-one. Well, he and his party went missing. No contact. The Chinese government says they couldn't find a trace of them."

"How big an expedition?"

"Just five. Vanished into the Gobi desert. Now the Chinese government have certified him and all the missing as dead, but his wife won't accept it. She wants to send a party in to find him. One that will stay under the Chinese radar. She wants someone who knows paleontology and knows Professor Carson. That person will know where to look for him. That person is you."

"I would love to help, really, but I can't leave in the middle of the semester."

"Arrangements have all been made. Private jets, expert guides. You'll be back before your afternoon class the Monday after Thanksgiving break."

Grant didn't have anything planned for the Thanksgiving break. And he owed Professor Carson more than he could ever repay.

"I can do that," Grant said.

"Excellent."

The lawyer reached into his bag and pulled out a sealed legal sized envelope with Grant's name handwritten on the outside. Grant recognized Professor Carson's writing immediately. He'd seen enough of it scribbled over every research paper he'd written.

"The professor left this for you," the lawyer said, "in the event anything went wrong during his expedition."

"What's in it?"

"No idea. I was legally bound to deliver it unopened. A car will be by your house to pick you up at five PM."

The lawyer shook Grant's hand and then closed his bag and headed for the door.

"There have been so many new discoveries coming out of China," Grant called after him. "Any idea what he was searching for?"

"I'm no scientist," the lawyer said over his shoulder. "And he must have been using a nickname for whatever it was. He kept telling his wife he was looking for dragons."

The End

AFTERWORD

Grant and Janaina were in a hell of a mess at the end of *Monsters in the Clouds*, lost in the upper reaches of the Amazon. I couldn't just leave them there. But on the other hand, I couldn't just let them float on home. Rainforests have snakes. Ancient rainforests had giant snakes. A story was born.

What's real within this fiction? The Aztec Empire for one. From the 1400s until the 1500s a collection of city-states all lived under a federation centrally administered by the Aztec King. They built great cities all throughout Central America. There are many that have been rediscovered out in the rainforests. The ones closer to civilization attract tourists. The ones less accessible attract scholars. It is unlikely that any of the cities were actually as far south as northern Brazil, but my Viper King would have to live at the empire's edge, so his fictional city is way out there.

King Axayacatl ruled the empire from 1469 to 1481. He did have two brothers, but my fictional half-brother Tizcatl was not one of them.

Spiders figure in a great deal of ancient artwork in the Americas, especially the Moche people in Peru. The Nazca culture even depicted a giant spider on the Nazca plains. Were there giant spiders? There's no proof there ever were. But hey, there's no proof there *never* were, right?

The spiders in this story are modeled after ground spiders. They do not spin conventional webs, but dig holes and spin webs within them. They hunt by ambush from these concealed positions and are not big climbers. Some of these species are also spitting spiders, a species that actually do spit bits of venomous webbing to immobilize their prey. Want to know something really scary? There are over a hundred different species of spiders that can spit webbing.

In the story, the Viper King has these giant spiders under his control. Not sure how smart or trainable small spiders are, but I'm giving the bigger spiders with bigger brains a lot of benefit of the doubt on being smarter. The characters reference Hannibal, a Carthaginian general who employed elephants as war machines around 216 B.C. They were splendid terror weapons against some crack Roman legions, though I doubt their service was voluntary. Hannibal and his life story is a great Internet rabbit hole to wander down when you have some free time.

How about that giant snake? Well, *Titanoboa* was an actual snake from about 60 million years ago. It grew to an estimated 13 meters long (42 feet) and weighed about 1,135 kilograms or 2,500 pounds. That's a major snake. But it likely killed by constriction, which is way too slow for such a short novel, so my snake is a cross with a venomous pit viper. Snakes do go into periods of hibernation, called brumation, like the giant viper in the story. Garter, queen, and corn snakes specifically do it, just not for hundreds of years.

A big, heartfelt thanks goes out to Donna Fitzpatrick, Deb Grace, Janet Guy, and Paul Siluch who all Beta read this story and helped me find the plot holes, typos, and inconsistencies that I seem to excel at. Thank you, all you wonderful people.

And at the 2018 Los Angeles Festival of Books, I inscribed a copy of one of Grant Coleman's adventures to a pretty little girl who had to spell her name for me. Her father told me it was Aztec for star. So, Citlali, the warrior leader defending the pyramid is named after you.

So this adventure wraps up a trilogy for Professor Grant Coleman. Will he sign up and go hunt for dragons in China? We'll have to see.

For him, stranger things have happened.

-Russell James
May 2018

CHECK OUT OTHER GREAT HORROR NOVELS

MONSTROSITY
by Tim Curran

The Food. It seeped from the ground, a living, gushing, teratogenic nightmare. It contaminated anything that ate it, causing nature to run wild with horrible mutations, creating massive monstrosities that roam the land destroying towns and cities, feeding on livestock and human beings and one another. Now Frank Bowman, an ordinary farmer with no military skills, must get his children to safety. And that will mean a trip through the contaminated zone of monsters, madmen, and The Food itself. Only a fool would attempt it. Or a man with a mission.

THE SQUIRMING
by Jack Hamlyn

You are their hosts.

You are their food.

The parasites came out of nowhere, squirming horrors that enslaved the human race. They turned the population into mindless pack animals, psychotic cannibalistic hordes whose only purpose was to feed them.

Now with the human race teetering at the edge of extinction, extermination teams are fighting back, killing off the parasites and their voracious hosts. Taking them out one by one in violent, bloody encounters.

The future of mankind is at stake.

And time is running out.

CHECK OUT OTHER GREAT
HORROR NOVELS

BLACK FRIDAY
by Michael Hodges

Jared the kleptomaniac, Chike the unemployed IT guy, Patricia the shopaholic, and Jeff the meth dealer are trapped inside a Chicago supermall on Black Friday. Bridgefield Mall empties during a fire alarm, and most of the shoppers drive off into a strange mist surrounding the mall parking lot. They never return. Chike and his group try calling friends and family, but their smart phones won't work, not even Twitter. As the mist creeps closer, the mall lights flicker and surge. Bulbs shatter and spray glass into the air. Unsettling noises are heard from within the mist, as the meth dealer becomes unhinged and hunts the group within the mall. Cornered by the mist, and hunted from within, Chike and the survivors must fight for their lives while solving the mystery of what happened to Bridgefield Mall. Sometimes, a good sale just isn't worth it.

GRIMWEAVE
by Tim Curran

In the deepest, darkest jungles of Indochina, an ancient evil is waiting in a forgotten, primeval valley. It is patient, monstrous, and bloodthirsty. Perfectly adapted to its hot, steaming environment, it strikes silent and stealthy, it chosen prey: human. Now Michael Spiers, a Marine sniper, the only survivor of a previous encounter with the beast, is going after it again. Against his better judgement, he is made part of a Marine Force Recon team that will hunt it down and destroy it.

The hunters are about to become the hunted.

CHECK OUT OTHER GREAT HORROR NOVELS

DEATH CRAWLERS
by Gerry Griffiths

Worldwide, there are thought to be 8,000 species of centipede, of which, only 3,000 have been scientifically recorded. The venom of Scolopendra gigantea—the largest of the arthropod genus found in the Amazon rainforest—is so potent that it is fatal to small animals and toxic to humans. But when a cargo plane departs the Amazon region and crashes inside a national park in the United States, much larger and deadlier creatures escape the wreckage to roam wild, reproducing at an astounding rate. Entomologist, Frank Travis solicits small town sheriff Wanda Rafferty's help and together they investigate the crash site. But as a rash of gruesome deaths befalls the townsfolk of Prospect, Frank and Wanda will soon discover how vicious and cunning these new breed of predators can be. Meanwhile, Jake and Nora Carver, and another backpacking couple, are venturing up into the mountainous terrain of the park. If only they knew their fun-filled weekend is about to become a living nightmare.

THE PULLER
by Michael Hodges

Matt Kearns has two choices: fight or hide. The creature in the orchard took the rest. Three days ago, he arrived at his favorite place in the world, a remote shack in Michigan's Upper Peninsula. The plan was to mourn his father's death and figure out his life. Now he's fighting for it. An invisible creature has him trapped. Every time Matt tries to flee, he's dragged backwards by an unseen force. Alone and with no hope of rescue, Matt must escape the Puller's reach. But how do you free yourself from something you cannot see?

Made in United States
Orlando, FL
03 February 2022

14402449R00086